The Secret at Sunset Hill

K.T. McGivens

K. T. McGivens

ISBN: 978-1-69-234665-2

DEDICATION

To Nancy Drew

Legendary fictional detective
who continues to inspire generations of readers.

CONTENTS

CHAPTER 1
THE ASSIGNMENT

The wind blew through Katie Porter's light brown hair as she sped along in her brand new 1947 MG convertible. It was a birthday present from her parents and had just arrived from England.

"So terribly sorry that we can't be there for your twenty-first, dear one, but we hope you like this little present. Love, Mom and Pa," said the note that came with the car.

"Just their way of buying your love," replied her grandmother, stiffly, as she handed back the note. "You would think that your parents would have at least made the effort to come home for your twenty-first birthday."

The Porters were world travelers and were seldom home. In fact, Katie could not remember the last time she laid eyes on them. Currently, they were in the depths of Asia tracking tigers, climbing a mountain, or meditating with a Buddhist monk. One could never be sure. They had ordered the car as they passed through London. Her birthday was still a week away, but Katie didn't mind that her present had arrived early.

"Now, Gran," replied Katie, her blue eyes twinkling as she smiled. "You know how they are. Besides, it's a lovely present! I shall enjoy it immensely!"

She arrived at the newspaper office just before noon and spun into a parking spot close to the front door. After glancing at herself in the rearview mirror to adjust her hat, she stepped from the MG and closed the car door carefully behind her.

"I'm just in time," she told herself. "Now to tackle the bear."

The "bear" was Tom Conner, editor of the *Fairfield Gazette*, with whom she had an appointment in five minutes. She hoped to secure a position with the newspaper. Mr. Conner was an old Army buddy of her father's, but he wasn't going to hand her a job just because of that. She knew she would have to prove herself.

"Mr. Conner will be with you in a moment," said the secretary from behind an L-shaped desk just outside the editor's door. "Please take a seat."

As Katie sat down, she glanced around the room. It was enclosed by glass walls on two sides so that one could see the outer room of reporters hovering over their typewriters and telephones. She had walked through the clamor of that outer room, drawing looks from the reporters and even a few whistles, but once the door of the editor's reception room had closed, the noise had been blocked out and it was quiet where she now sat.

The room was furnished in a tastefully modern style which was somewhat surprising so soon after the end of the war, with several beautifully painted landscapes hanging on the solid inner walls.

"Mr. Conner paints," explained the gray-haired secretary, noticing Katie's gaze. "You may go in now."

"Thank you," replied Katie, standing. "He's very good," she added over her shoulder as she opened the editor's door.

"Ah, there you are!" greeted Tom Conner, pushing his chair away from his desk and standing. "You must be Katie Porter. Sorry to keep you waiting!"

He was a rather large man, middle aged, with dark brown hair that was beginning to gray at the temples. He was in his shirt sleeves, rolled up to the elbows, and the knot in his tie was loosened at the collar. Despite his somewhat disheveled appearance, there was a gentle attractiveness about him, and Katie had the fleeting impression of a man who smoked a pipe and sipped Scotch in his off hours.

He took a few steps towards her and shook her hand.

"Yes," she replied. "Thank you so much for agreeing to see me."

"Sure, sure," replied Mr. Conner, motioning her to the chair in front of his desk, as he returned to his own seat. "Anything for Capt. Porter. I imagine you know that your father and I served together in the war?" and when Katie nodded, continued. "So, what can I do for you, young lady?"

"Well, it was actually my father who suggested that I stop by and talk to you about the possibility of joining your staff," answered Katie, politely.

"Really?" said the editor, glancing down at a stack of papers in front of him. "We don't have any secretarial positions open now, but perhaps Mrs. Mathers could find something for you in Reception or as a telephone operator."

"I beg your pardon, Mr. Connor," responded Katie. "But there seems to be a bit of a misunderstanding. As nice as those positions sound, I'm here for a reporter's position. I understand that the *Gazette* lost several reporters during the war and has vacancies. I believe that I am fully qualified to fill one of those."

"You're kidding, right?" replied Tom Conner, looking up suddenly. "But you're a … well, what are your qualifications? What experience do you have? Miss Porter, we are a very serious operation here and only hire the best candidates. I only took your appointment because you're Capt. Porter's daughter. You are wasting your time and mine."

"Mr. Connor," countered Katie, remaining unflustered. "I am a college educated journalist. I was a reporter, and then editor, of my college newspaper. I have covered many serious stories," she added, taking an envelope from her purse. "Here is a sampling of my work along with my resume. How am I going to gain the necessary experience if I can't get hired by a professional outfit like the *Fairfield Gazette*?"

As she started to hand the envelope over to the reluctant editor, his door suddenly flew open and an angry young man came marching into the room with Mr. Connor's secretary following close on his heels.

"I tried to stop him, Mr. Connor, but he just pushed passed me," she said.

"That's quite all right, Mrs. Mathers," replied the editor, with a wave of his hand. "I'll handle this."

As the secretary retreated, Tom Connor took charge of the young man. "What's this all about, Butler?"

"You have no right!" cried the young man, his handsome face growing red. "I've been waiting for weeks to cover the White debutant party! It's the biggest, most exclusive, event of the year and you've given it to Midge Pennington who couldn't tell the difference between a chocolate eclair and a Claire Cardell!"

"A what?" replied a confused Mr. Connor.

"One is delicious with coffee and the other I'm wearing right now," interrupted Katie, standing to extend her hand out to Mr. Butler.

"Oh! I do beg your pardon!" said the startled young man, turning around and reaching to shake her hand. "I didn't see you there. And, yes, that Cardell dress you're wearing is lovely!" he said, giving her outfit an appreciative look.

"Thank you," replied Katie.

"Miss Katie Porter, please allow me to introduce Mr. E.M. Butler," said Mr. Connor. "E.M., this is Miss Porter."

"A pleasure to meet you," Katie and E.M. said in unison, nodding to each other.

"Look, E.M.," Tom Connor continued. "Midge needs the story and, besides, she's a woman."

"The fact that she's a woman is quite obvious," Mr. Butler huffed. "But I fail to see the relevance to her getting the story over me. I usually cover the social events for this newspaper. Midge covers women's sports."

"I just think that a woman would cover this debutante thing better," argued the editor. "Midge may be more easily accepted into the party, better able to get the inside scoop."

"Wait a minute!" said Katie. "You're not talking about Boots White's party, are you? The one being held at Sunset Hill this weekend?"

"Yes, that's the one," replied E.M.

"Why, I've got an invitation!" exclaimed Katie. "Boots' older sister, Ruth, and I are best friends. And I'm able to bring a guest!"

Tom Connor and E.M. Butler turned to look at her in surprise.

"It's a shame that I don't work for the *Fairfield Gazette*," she said with a sigh, plopping back down in her chair. "I could write an exclusive story on the party and bring Mr. Butler here along as my guest to make sure it was up to *Gazette* editorial standards."

E.M. Butler let out a soft choking sound, a look of hope in his eyes, as he turned to his editor.

"Well?" he managed to say to Mr. Connor.

Tom Connor stood silently for a moment, running the situation through his mind. This was a big story. Could he really take a chance on this young woman, even with E.M. by her side?

"O.K." he finally replied. "You've both got the story. But don't screw it up or so help me!"

"Wonderful!" exclaimed Katie, standing to join E.M. in the middle of the room.

"We won't let you down, Mr. Conner!" promised E.M. "Will we, Miss Porter?"

"Absolutely not!" replied Katie.

"Now what am I going to do with Midge Pennington?" sighed Tom Connor, scratching his head. "She's going to be very upset!"

"Does Miss Pennington ride, by any chance?" asked Katie, reaching for her purse.

"Yes, I think so," replied Mr. Conner. "Why?"

"Well, I happen to know that there's to be a women's only cross-country equestrian race at the Rosegate Estate on Saturday. A bunch of socialites and celebrities will be participating. Might the *Gazette* be interested in Miss Pennington covering that story?"

"Yes, I believe so," agreed the editor, relieved. "I'll reassign her. Who should she contact, Miss Porter, to get an invitation?"

"Leave that to me," replied Katie. "I'll see that she gets one," and, with that, she left the room with E.M. Butler close behind her.

"Do you really think you can get Midge into the Rosegate Estate?" he asked, as they made their way back through the reporters' room and out into the hallway. "I'm glad that we wrestled the White story away from her, but I like Midge and know that she really needs an assignment."

"Oh, that's no problem," replied Katie, rifling through her purse for her car keys as she opened the front door and walked out into the afternoon sunlight. "I happen to live there with my grandmother."

"Really?" exclaimed E.M. Butler, in surprise.

"Yes," she answered. "Now all I have to do is organize a women's only cross-country equestrian race for this Saturday."

She waved as she drove away, leaving the startled young man standing on the sidewalk. "I believe that pretty young woman and I are going to be great friends!" thought E.M. smiling to himself. "Yes, indeed!"

As previously arranged, early on Saturday morning, Katie once again swung into the parking lot of the *Gazette* but this time it was to pick up E.M. who was waiting for her in the lobby.

He was immaculately dressed in a black suit and gray vest. A white carnation adorned his lapel, and he carried a fancy cane. A small suitcase and larger suit bag rested on a bench nearby. He stood and tipped his Fedora to Katie as she entered the building.

"Good morning, Miss Porter," he said in greeting. "As you can see, I'm ready to go!"

"Yes, indeed," replied Katie. "I hope I haven't kept you waiting?"

"Not at all," said E.M., tucking the cane under an arm as he reached for his luggage.

"Please allow me to help, Mr. Butler," said Katie, taking the suitcase from him. "My car is right outside."

As they walked out of the building and toward the parking lot, they nodded to several *Gazette* employees arriving for work at the newspaper.

"The weekend shift," replied E.M. to Katie's puzzled look.

"Yes, of course," she answered. "I suppose the news never takes a weekend off."

"No, indeed," was his only response.

She opened the back compartment of the little car where her bags were already stowed. She tucked E.M.'s suitcase next to hers, and then took his cane so that he could lay the larger suit bag across the other luggage.

"War injury?" observed Katie, holding it up before securing it between their bags.

"Only to my ego," replied E.M., softly. "The cane is for effect. I came out of the war unscathed."

Katie only nodded and smiled, as she put the MG in gear and pulled away from the curb.

"I telephoned my friend Ruth to let her know that I'm bringing a guest," said Katie as she expertly navigated the narrow roads of Fairview on their way out of town. The Sunset Hill estate was approximately 10 miles north of the city and sat up on a hill surrounded by an expanse of acreage.

"Good idea," agreed E.M., nodding. "And how did you describe me to your friend?"

"I left it a bit vague," she replied. "I wanted to give us a chance to come up with something."

"Did you mention that I'm a reporter with the *Gazette*?" asked E.M., gazing out at the countryside whizzing by.

"Heavens, no!" exclaimed Katie. "That will put everyone on their guard. We want to get a 'this is how the rich really lives' story, don't we?"

"Well, yes," replied E.M. "But won't your friend, Ruth, be upset when she finds out?"

"Not if I pass it by her before we print it," said Katie, taking a corner rather fast. E.M. gripped the car door and held onto his hat.

"Hum, censorship," murmured E.M. "I'm not sure I like that, Miss Porter."

"No, it's not really," replied Katie, shooting him a glance. "Ruthie's alright, you'll see. If fact, I believe that she'll be a real help to us."

They continued their discussion of the White family, whom Katie appeared to know well, until Sunset Hill appeared on the horizon.

"There it is!" exclaimed Katie, pointing in the direction of the mansion sitting high on a hill. Within minutes they were turning through the large metal gates that marked the entrance and driving up the long driveway.

"What a driveway! I hope we arrive before I hit retirement age," joked E.M.

"Well that depends on how old you are now," shot back Katie with a chuckle, turning the car toward the front of the house and gliding to a stop at the walkway leading to the front door.

A large solemn looking man, dressed in a dark suit and bowtie, came out and walked gracefully down the walkway. Stepping out behind him and waiting a few feet up the walkway was a young woman of about Katie's age.

"Good morning, Miss Katie," said the man, opening her car door and bowing slightly.

"Good morning, Ambrose," replied Katie, stepping out of the MG. "How are you?"

"Very well, Miss, thank you," replied the butler, closing the door behind her, and walking around the front of the vehicle to open the passenger side door for E.M., who was already halfway out.

"Katie!" cried the young woman, walking toward her and reaching out to give Katie a hug. "I'm so glad that you could come!"

"I wouldn't miss Boots' debutante party for the world," exclaimed Katie, wrapping her arm around her friend's waist and turning slightly. "Please allow me to introduce our new friend, Mr. E.M. Butler," she added, nodding to E.M. as he approached the two young women.

Ruth White extended her hand and graciously shook his. "Hello, Mr. Butler. I'm Ruth White. I'm delighted to meet you," she said. "I'm so glad that you could join us."

Ruth White was an extraordinarily beautiful woman. Tall and slender, she had golden blond hair and sparkling blue eyes, with a hint of freckles across the bridge of her nose. Her warm smile revealed dimples on each cheek, and she wore a light summer dress, beige in color, simple but expensively made and a necklace around her neck with a locket attached. E.M. was to discover, much later, that it contained the picture of her fiancé, Robert.

"Miss White," replied E.M., taken aback somewhat, by the grandeur that surrounded him. "The pleasure is all mine! Thank you so much for allowing me to join the party."

They proceeded up the walkway with Ambrose following behind carrying their luggage. Just as they approached the open front door, they heard a voice shouting down at them from high above.

"Beware! Beware!" the voice shrilled loudly. "You're going to die! Die!"

CHAPTER 2
MYSTERIOUS VISITORS

E.M. Butler froze in his tracks and looked over at Katie, waiting for her signal to either duck or run. Katie, however, was not alarmed and had turned to look upward.

"I believe he's up there, Ruthie," she observed, motioning in the direction of a nearby tree. "In the top of that tree."

"Oh dear," sighed Ruth, and turning to the butler. "Ambrose, please let Mr. Tom know that Mad Uncle Henry has escaped again and is up in the tree. We can't have him shouting down at our guests as they arrive."

"Yes, Miss Ruth," replied Ambrose, shooting an annoyed glance up at the treetop. "Immediately".

E.M. pulled himself together and followed the women inside the mansion wondering to himself what kind of asylum Katie Porter had brought him to.

They entered a large foyer, then walked through the great hall, and up one of the two grand staircases that bordered on either side. Stopping on the landing, Ruth turned to E.M. and, placing a hand gently on his arm, said, "Mr. Butler, Ambrose will show you to your room. Katie and I will be in hers, three doors down on the left. Let's meet in ten minutes and go down to meet Mother together."

"Great idea," replied E.M. and turned to follow Ambrose down the hall as Ruth and Katie continued in the other direction.

"What a lovely young man!" commented Ruth White, as they entered Katie's room and closed the door behind them. "Where did the two of you meet?"

She sat on the edge of the bed as Katie changed into a more suitable outfit for luncheon.

"In the editor's office of the *Fairfield Gazette*," replied Katie, calmly. "He's a colleague."

"Katie!" exclaimed her friend. "You got the job at the newspaper!"

"Yes!" laughed Katie, grabbing both of Ruth's hands and giving them a gentle squeeze. "I got the job! I had to do some fancy footwork but here I am! Boots' party is my first assignment."

"You mean, the paper sent you here to do a story?" asked Ruth, somewhat shocked. "But you were invited as our guest. Mother's not going to like this."

"No, silly," replied Katie. "I *am* here as your invited guest. And as your friend. But I also talked Mr. Connor into letting me use the opportunity to prove to the paper that I can cover an important event. I'm not going to print anything that you will find objectionable. In fact, you can help me write the article!"

"Well, I don't know," said Ruth, nervously. But she knew her friend all too well. "I suppose it would be useless to talk you out of this, correct?"

"Correct," exclaimed Katie, giving Ruth a quick hug. "But just to play it safe, I don't think we should tell your family. It's better that E.M. and I remain undercover."

"You really are incorrigible!" Ruth replied, chuckling, as she stood to respond to a knock on the bedroom door. She opened it to reveal E.M. standing in the hallway, hat in hand.

"Oh, good!" he exclaimed. "I was afraid I might have the wrong room! This place is like a labyrinth, where I need a map to find my way around."

"It's not that bad," chuckled Ruth, reaching out and pulling him into the room. "It only took me ten years to find my way around, but, then again, I was born here!" she teased.

"We've been plotting our next move," said Katie to E.M. "I think that you and I should remain undercover so that we can write the article we want. But Ruthie is claiming review rights."

"Well, I suppose that's fair," sighed E.M., dramatically. "After all, it's her house and her sister's party!"

"Speaking of the party," recalled Katie. "Who's on the guest list? Anyone we don't know?"

"Let's see," replied Ruth, thoughtfully. "There will be the usual suspects, of course. About fifty people in all. Mother and Father insisted that it be small this time, since it's so soon after the war ended," she added.

"Hum, yes," agreed Katie. "Too bad, really. I remember that there were at least one hundred guests at your debutante party, most of whom ended up in the fountain by the end of the evening," she added, chuckling.

"Yes, well," said Ruth, seriously. "The family wanted to avoid that scenario this time around."

Katie gathered up her scarf and, throwing it around her neck, led them to the door and back out into the hallway.

"You know," began Ruth, again. "I nearly forgot but two friends of Ruddy's will be here, as well. Kenneth West and James Fielding. Former comrades in arms, I believe. They're in town and asked if they could stop by. We invited them to the party since two more people won't make any difference."

"Ruddy?" E.M. silently mouthed to Katie, raising his eyebrows.

She shook her head and mouthed back, "later," as they continued down to the living room where the family and a few other guests had gathered to await the call to lunch.

"Katie!" exclaimed Ruth's mother. "How nice to see you again."

"It's wonderful to see you, Mrs. White," returned Katie, greeting the older woman with a hug, and turning back slightly, added. "Please allow me to introduce my friend, Mr. E.M. Butler."

"A pleasure to meet you, Mr. Butler," replied Mrs. White, stepping forward and extending her hand.

"The pleasure is all mine," responded E.M., giving Ruth's mother a slight bow as he shook her hand. "Thank you for letting me barge into your beautiful home."

"You are very welcome, Mr. Butler," replied Mrs. White. "Any friend of Katie's is welcome here."

Ruth led the pair around the room, making further introductions. Many already knew Katie, of course, and greeted her with hugs and handshakes. E.M. was greeted warmly but with less enthusiasm.

"This is my sister, Margaret," Ruth said as she introduced E.M. to a thin blushing girl standing in the corner. "We call her Boots. It's her party that you'll be attending this evening."

"Un Plaisir, mademoiselle!" said E.M. to Boots, as he gently shook her hand. "Congratulations on your big day!"

"Le Plaisir est pour moi," returned Boots, with a shy smile, before dropping her gaze to the floor.

"Charmer," teased Katie, giving E.M. a poke in the ribs as she scooted past him to give Boots a warm hug. "Hello, Boots! Are you nervous about tonight?"

"Yes, a little," replied the young woman, nodding. "There'll be so many people!"

"Giving you ample opportunity to duck out and hide if things should get too overwhelming," laughed Katie.

"Don't tell her that," scolded Ruth, but she was smiling. "It's taken us more than a year to convince Boots that she needs a debutante party at all!"

"A torture we men don't have to endure," said a voice from across the room.

"Tom! I didn't see you hiding over there," exclaimed Katie, crossing the room to embrace Ruth's brother. "How are you? Were you able to grab Mad Uncle Henry?"

"No, he managed to stay just out of my reach!" replied Tom White. "But he'll get hungry soon."

"Tom, this is my friend, Mr. E.M. Butler," said Katie, introducing the two men. "Mr. Butler, this is Thomas White, Ruthie and Boots' wayward brother."

"And Katie's future husband," added Tom, with a wink.

"Really?" asked E.M., looking from Tom to Katie.

"Don't believe a word of it," Katie replied calmly, giving Tom a disapproving look. "It's just wishful thinking on Tom's part."

At that moment, Ambrose entered the room and announced that lunch was ready. The group strolled across the hall and into the large dining room. Since lunch was an informal affair, guests were encouraged to sit where they chose, and Katie slid into the chair next to Boots. Mrs. White, of course, sat at one end of the table but the chair at its head remained empty.

"Where's Poppy today?" Katie asked Boots, as she laid her napkin across her lap. "Isn't he joining us for lunch?"

Poppy was Ruth's father, the Honorable James White, head of the family and esteemed Judge in Fairfield. He had the distinction of being the direct descendant of the man who had once been the British Regional Governor of the state in the 1770's and the original owner of Sunset Hill, Ogden White. Fortunately for the lineage, when the Revolutionary War broke out, Ogden decided to side with the American rebels, thus saving life, limb, and property. His descendant, James, was a well-liked, easy-going, affable man. He was adored by his children who, somewhere through the years, started calling him "Poppy." Since Katie had spent so much of her youth at the estate that she was considered a member of the family, she called Judge White 'Poppy' as well.

"No," replied Boots. "He sent a note from town saying that he is tied up at a city council meeting. He'll most likely grab something to eat at City Hall."

"So, Mr. Butler," asked Tom from across the table. "What do the initials E.M. stand for?"

"I don't actually know," replied E.M., smiling over at Tom. "It's a secret that my parents never shared with me."

Tom narrowed his eyes and persisted. "No need to be flippant, Mr. Butler," he said stiffly. "If you're embarrassed about your name, you should just say so."

"You're being rude, Tom," said Ruth, shooting a withering look at her brother and then turning to E.M., who was seated next to her. "Please excuse my brother, Mr. Butler, apparently he's left his manners with the goats this morning."

"At least we don't name our goats with initials," muttered Tom under his breath as he took a bite of his lunch.

"Katie," interceded Mrs. White, quickly changing the subject. "How long have you and Mr. Butler known each other? How did you meet?"

"Er…well…," Katie began with a struggle. She mentally chided herself for not taking the time to coordinate a plausible story with E.M. They were supposed to come up with something on their drive to the estate that morning but never got around to it. Now she was stuck.

"They ran into each other in the Fairfield park, mother," replied Ruth, saving her friend. "If I recall the story correctly, Katie, Mr. Butler helped you retrieve Nugget from the pond."

"Yes!" replied a relieved Katie. "Nugget got away from me and jumped right into the water. I was fearful that he would drown but Mr. Butler was there to save the day. He waded in and pulled him out."

"You needn't have gotten wet, Mr. Butler," said Boots, in a matter-of-fact tone, as she dug her fork into her chicken salad. "Yorkies can swim."

"Yes, of course," nodded E.M., joining in on the fib. "I just thought it the gallant thing to do since Miss Porter seemed so distressed at seeing the little fellow in the water."

"That dog runs wild, Katie," replied Mrs. White, sternly. "You must really get him some obedience training."

At that moment, the dining room door swung open and Ambrose entered, loudly announcing, "Mr. Kenneth West and Mr. James Fielding!"

Ruth stood and crossed the room to greet the two visitors as they entered. Mr. Kenneth West was the first to reach Ruth and shake her hand.

"You must be Miss White," he said with a warm smile. "I'm Kenneth West. Thank you so very much for allowing us to crash your sister's debutante party! It was very nice of you!"

Kenneth West was a pleasant looking young man of about twenty-five years old with cropped blond hair and an athletic build. He was very tall, with large hands, and Ruth's hand completely disappeared as she shook his.

"You are very welcome, Mr. West," she replied. "We're delighted to have you."

As attractive as Mr. West was, his companion was even more so. Like his friend, he had an athletic build, but more like a swimmer, with broad shoulders and well-defined arms. He had light brown hair and blue eyes, which sparkled as he glanced around the room. His broad smile was warm and engaging and definitely his best feature. Katie heard small gasps from both Boots and E.M.

"This is Jim Fielding," said Kenneth, turning to introduce him to Ruth. "He also served with your brother."

"Hello Mr. Fielding," replied Ruth, shaking his hand. "Welcome. Please let me introduce you both to my mother," she added, leading the men over to the table.

After introductions were made to Mrs. White and the others, Mr. West and Mr. Fielding were encouraged to sit down and join the group for lunch and they readily accepted. There was an empty chair next to E.M. and Kenneth West strolled over to take it. Jim Fielding found a chair next to Tom White.

"So, Mr. Fielding," Tom began. "I understand that you served in the 1st Infantry Division with my brother Ruddy." When Jim nodded, Tom asked, "What Regiment?

"The 16th," replied Jim, taking a sip from his glass.

"Then you must have participated in Operation Musketeer," continued Tom. "My brother wrote us all about it."

"I believe you're mistaken," corrected Jim. "Operation Musketeer was in the Pacific, as part of the campaign to liberate the Philippines. Your brother and I fought in the European theatre. Sicily and then Omaha Beach. I can show you my orders if you need proof," he added with a disarming smile.

"I'm sure that won't be necessary," interjected Katie, who had sat in rapt attention, listening to the exchange. "But in Tom's defense, one can't be too careful these days."

"Agreed," smiled Jim, turning to give her an intense gaze. "One can never be too careful."

Katie wasn't quite sure what to make of him. She knew that she was probably blushing, something she didn't often do, so she dropped her head down to concentrate on the food on her plate.

"What on earth is wrong with me," she thought to herself, fighting to regain her senses. "I don't know this man. I refuse to be taken in by him, charming smile and all!"

The rest of the meal turned to less inflammatory talk and soon broke up so that guests could rest before changing for the big party that was to start at seven o'clock. Cocktails would be available at six for those who wished to imbibe.

E.M. grabbed Katie by the elbow and led her outside and onto the back patio.

"I think I know that gentleman," he whispered, leaning toward her.

'Which one?" replied Katie, pretending not to understand.

"Jim Fielding, that's which one," he replied. "I believe he works as a reporter for the *Middleton Times*!"

"Our competitor?" she replied, raising her eyebrows and gazing over her shoulder to make sure they weren't being overhead.

"Yes, our competitor!" exclaimed E.M. "But Fielding usually covers political stories. I can't imagine why he would be here at a debutant party."

"Perhaps he really is only here as Ruddy's friend," Katie wondered.

"And not as a reporter."

"I think I'd better call a friend of mine at the *Times* just to make sure," said E.M. "Mary once dated Jim Fielding. Perhaps she can tell us what he's up to!"

"Sounds good!" agreed Katie. "In the meantime, I think I'll do a little spying. I'll see you later!"

She left E.M. to make his call and went in search of Jim Fielding and Kenneth West. She spotted them walking across the expansive back yard toward the large fountain. They appeared to be in deep conversation.

There was no place for her to hide as she followed them, so she was forced to remain at quite a distance behind them. Unfortunately, this meant that she could not hear what they were saying but their actions seemed to indicate that they were not just out for a stroll.

When they reached the fountain, the two men circled the structure twice, examining it intently as they went around, before stopping to sit at its edge. Katie approached slowly and as quietly, as she could, hoping to delay the inevitability of being seen. She was about one hundred yards from the fountain when a loud scream rang out from the house and drifted across the yard, followed by the shouts, "Help! Help! I've been robbed!" .

CHAPTER 3
STRANGE OCCURRENCES

Katie spun around and started running in the direction of the mansion. The two men who she had been following joined her, catching up and passing Katie halfway up the lawn. All three arrived to find Boots standing in the hallway, an open jewelry case in her hand.

"Someone's stolen my pearl necklace and two of my rings!" she cried, holding up the case.

Katie took the case from her and examined it. It was indeed empty and it looked as though the lock had been forced open.

"Do you usually keep this locked?" she asked Boots.

"No," replied the girl, brushing tears from her face. "There's never been a need. No one here would steal and, besides, the lock has been broken for ages."

"When was the last time you opened the case?" asked Jim Fielding, looking over Katie's shoulder.

"I don't know," replied Boots, looking up at him. "I can't remember. I think, perhaps, when I attended the Opera. That would have been over a week ago."

"Well, that means that the necklace and rings could have been taken at any time during the last week," remarked Kenneth West, somewhat casually.

"Yes," replied Katie, looking directly at him. "Including today."

"Perhaps we should search Miss Boots' room," advised Jim. "To make sure the jewels didn't fall out accidently and roll under something."

Despite Boots' argument that she was always very careful in the handling of the case and was confident that the jewelry could not have fallen out, Katie and Jim started up the staircase toward Boots' bedroom.

Kenneth, however, stayed below stating that he did not feel comfortable intruding on the young lady's privacy.

"I don't think it proper for a man to be in a woman's boudoir when she is of no relation to him," he smiled after them.

"No, of course not," Katie sarcastically shot back over her shoulder, her eyebrows raised.

With Boots in tow, they met Ruth on the landing, who had been on her way to investigate the commotion.

"I'll ask Rosemary to help," she said, turning back down the hall and into one of the bedrooms where the housekeeper was removing some linen. Soon Katie, Jim, Boots, Ruth and Rosemary were searching Boots' bedroom for the missing necklace and rings. Sensitive to Boots' discomfort, Jim limited his actions to looking under the bed and other furniture, leaving the women to inspect the drawers and closets.

At one point, Katie glanced out of the bedroom window and saw Kenneth walking briskly back over the lawn in the direction of the fountain.

"He's up to something," murmured Katie to herself. "And I'm going to find out what it is!"

Their search revealed nothing and, as the group left the room, Ruth commented that she'd have to tell her mother.

"This is a terrible thing to happen," she added, closing her sister's bedroom door. "Just when the party is about to get underway."

"Yes," replied Katie. "And there are so many people in the house. So many suspects!"

"Shouldn't we be calling the police?" asked Jim, walking beside Katie, as they followed Ruth down the hallway.

"No, I don't think so," replied Ruth, after a moment. "I think mother will want to wait to see if there might be some other explanation. I, for one, am not entirely convinced that Boots' jewelry has been stolen. She may have misplaced them or lent them out. She can be so scattered at times!"

She continued down the hall, stopping to knock on her mother's door before disappearing inside.

Katie turned to Jim. "Did you and Mr. West arrive together this afternoon?" she asked him, trying to sound casual while gazing up at him intensely.

"Ah, so we're both suspects," replied Jim, smiling. "I suppose that's a fair question. Yes, we arrived here at Sunset Hill together but I drove my car and, on my way through town, stopped to pick up Kenneth at the train station in Fairfield."

"I'm not accusing you or Mr. West of anything," she replied evenly. "But your arrival is rather timely."

"As is yours, Miss Porter," he countered. "And Mr. Butler's. After all, the jewelry could have been taken long before we arrived."

"And may I ask what you were discussing down at the fountain?" she asked, trying to keep her composure although she could feel her frustration rising.

'No, you may not," he replied. "But perhaps you'll have better luck in finding out if you follow us more closely next time."

Before she could reply, he gave her a slight bow before turning and walking away.

"Well, of all the nerve," she said to herself, disturbed by the man's cavalier manner. "Maybe E.M. has found out something about him," she thought, as she moved down the hallway to his room.

"We're in luck, Miss Porter!" exclaimed E.M., as he welcomed Katie into his room. "Mary was a wealth of information!"

"Wonderful," replied Katie, taking a seat by the window. "She confirmed that Jim Fielding is a reporter?"

"Yes," he answered. "She said it sounded like him based on my description and that he was, indeed, a reporter for the *Middleton Times*. But she was surprised to hear that he was here at Sunset Hill. She knew that he was a friend of Ruddy White but the last she had heard was that he was chasing a story in New York City."

"Well, perhaps he's finished with his story and, since he was passing so close to Ruddy's home, he decided to stop in," said Katie, resting her chin in her hand. "But I do have to admit that there is something about his being here that I just find odd."

"Oh, yes?" replied E.M. "How so?"

"Well, for one thing," she responded. "He and Mr. West engaged in a very serious conversation down at the fountain, which is rather far from the house. They obviously did not want to be overheard."

"There's nothing strange about that," replied E.M. "People have private conversations all the time. It doesn't mean anything."

"I agree," Katie responded. "But they went through an awful lot of trouble. They walked around the fountain several times before they sat down to talk."

"Perhaps they were just admiring the beauty of the architecture," replied E.M. "Or they were looking for the presence of listening devices."

"My thought exactly," agreed Katie. "The latter, that is. Their conversation must have been very private indeed. What else did Mary tell you?"

"That as far as she knew, he is still single," replied E.M. with a grin.

"What does that have to do with anything?" asked Katie, puzzled. Once again, she found that she was blushing slightly.

"I can't imagine," answered E.M., with both a grin and a shrug. "But she really wanted us to know."

They sat quietly for a moment before E.M. cleared his throat and asked, "so, where is this Ruddy person everyone keeps mentioning? His wartime comrades are here to see him, and his younger sister is about to celebrate her entrance into society. Yet the young man remains elusive."

"He's in France. Colleville-sur-Mer," replied Katie, softly, gazing out the window.

"Colleville-sur-Mer?" repeated E.M. "What on earth is he doing there? There's nothing in Colleville-sur-Mer except…oh," he caught himself and stopped.

Katie finished for him. "Except the American cemetery."

"Oh, dear," replied E.M. "I'm terribly sorry. Did you know him well?"

"Yes, very," was all Katie said, and then she stood and smoothed down her skirt. "Well, I suppose I'd better get ready for the party. Do you drink, Mr. Butler?"

"Whenever possible," replied E.M., nodding and smiling warmly.

"Excellent!" Katie said, returning his smile. "Then I'll meet you for cocktails." She moved toward the door but before she left the room she turned and asked, "Mr. Butler? Would you do me a favor?"

"Anything, Miss Porter," replied E.M., standing and taking a few steps toward her.

"Would you please call me Katie?" she said. "Miss Porter sounds so formal."

"Only if you call me E.M.," he replied. "Mr. Butler is my father and he and I have never gotten along."

"Agreed," said Katie, nodding, and with a wave, she left the room.

An hour later, she was just finishing getting ready for the evening's festivities when there was a knock on the door and Ruth poked her head in.

"Katie? If you're nearly ready, mother wondered if you might stop by her room before going down," she asked.

"Oh dear," Katie replied, raising her eyebrows, and looking up at her friend as she clipped on an earring. "Surely I can't be in trouble already?"

"No, nothing like that," replied Ruth, smiling. "See you in five minutes?"

"Yes," answered Katie. "I'll be there."

Giving herself one last look in the mirror, she closed the door behind her and walked down the hallway to Mrs. White's room. Once there, she knocked gently and called out, "Mrs. White?"

"Come in, Katie dear," was the reply and Katie opened the door to find the entire White family waiting for her.

"Happy Birthday, Katie!" they all shouted at once and Ruth rushed forward to pull the stunned girl into the room, closing the door behind them.

"Oh my!" was all that Katie could say, her mouth dropping open.

Ruth, who still held her by the elbow, chuckled and repeated, "Happy Birthday, dear Katie! We know that your birthday isn't until tomorrow, but the entire White family wanted to wish you a very happy birthday. I'll still be joining you and your grandmother for luncheon tomorrow to celebrate."

"That's very sweet," replied Katie, somewhat embarrassed and looking around at everyone. "But really not necessary."

"Of course, it is!" said Judge White, stepping over to give her a big hug and kiss on the cheek, as did the rest of the family, one by one.

"We know that one's twenty-first birthday is very special," said Mrs. White, handing Katie a small thin box beautifully wrapped. "So we hope that you will accept this small token as our gift to you from all of us."

"Oh!" exclaimed Katie, taking the box from Mrs. White. "How lovely, but you really shouldn't have gone to all the trouble!"

"Nonsense!" said the Judge, tucking his thumbs into his vest pockets. "Go ahead and open it!"

She carefully unwrapped it, and lifting the lid, looked down at a beautiful silver necklace with a locket attached.

"How lovely," she exclaimed. "Thank you!"

"Open it," Ruth whispered, pointing down at the locket. Her family appeared to hold their breaths as Katie lifted the necklace from the box and gently opened the locket. She looked at the picture inside for a moment before quickly snapping it shut.

"Don't you like it?" asked Boots, as Katie stood silently with her head down, the locket resting in the palm of her hand.

"Please forgive us if we've offended you…" began Mrs. White, anxiously, but Katie looked up and shook her head.

"No, no," she began, with tears in her eyes. "This is the most thoughtful…wonderful…," she paused, her voice catching in her throat. She stood for a moment fighting to regain her composure as she looked down again at the locket. Then, quickly wiping the tears from her face, she looked up again and continued, "this is the most precious gift you could have ever given me, and I shall treasure it always."

The family relaxed then as Katie added, "thank you so much, Mrs. White. Thank you, Poppy," giving them each a kiss on the cheek.

"Shall I help you put it on?" asked Tom, reaching out to take the necklace.

"Yes, please," replied Katie, handing it to him as he stepped around her. He deftly placed the necklace around her neck and snapped the clasp shut.

"Now to face our guests!" exclaimed Judge White, leading his family through the door.

Taking a quick glance in Mrs. White's mirror of herself wearing the locket, Katie joined the family as they proceeded downstairs.

About twenty people had gathered for cocktails in the drawing room.

Katie recognized Ann Gaston, a classmate of Boots, standing shyly by herself in a corner. She gave Katie a relieved smile as the older girl approached.

"Hello, Ann," Katie said in greeting. "It's so nice to see you. What is that you're drinking?"

"Sherry," replied Ann, raising her glass a little. "But I'm afraid I'm not enjoying it very much."

"Goodness," said Katie. "Why not? The Whites serve nothing but the best."

"Oh, it's not the fault of the sherry," Ann said quickly. "It's me. I'm not much of a drinker and sherry seemed like the safest bet."

"Yes, I suppose you're correct," replied Katie, smiling and taking a martini off of the tray offered her by Ambrose. "And one needs something in their hands if it's cocktail time."

She took a sip of her own drink and glanced around the room. There were several people she didn't recognize but she quickly picked out one of Ruth's former beaus chatting up a young blond girl leaning against the arm of the sofa as another girl giggled beside her. Edward had always been a notorious flirt and Katie was relieved when Ruth had finally broken things off with him.

Gazing past him, she could see Jim Fielding standing with Kenneth West, both with drinks in hand. They were seemingly studying a portrait on the wall with their backs to the rest of the room.

Katie watched them for a moment and then, excusing herself from Ann, strolled over.

"A wonderful piece, don't you think?" she said, coming to stand next to Kenneth. "But then again, Seurat's work is so brilliant."

"Yes, indeed," replied Kenneth. "Although I must admit that the impressionistic style is not one of my favorites. All those dots and dabs."

"Perhaps you're looking too closely," said Katie. "Impressionist's work is often best viewed at a distance."

"Like many things in life," smiled Jim. "One gets a better impression if one doesn't look too closely."

"I would say that depends on how one defines the term 'better'," replied Katie, looking directly into his eyes. "Things can appear to be real, at a distance, but may end up being only an illusion, like the figures in this painting."

"I agree," replied Jim, looking up again at the painting. "On the other hand, Miss Porter, sometimes the only way to gain clarity is to view things a few feet away. In this painting, are we looking at people enjoying a Sunday afternoon in the park or just a series of paint dots and dabs?"

"I hesitate to render an opinion," replied Katie. "I don't claim to be an art *aficionado*."

"You're being modest," said Jim, raising his eyebrows. "I believe you are more of an expert than you would have us believe."

"If you are referring to the truth, then yes, I confess that I'm usually anxious to find it," she replied.

Before Jim could respond they heard Ambrose announce, "Ladies and gentlemen! The party is about to begin. If you would please join the family in the main hall!"

The main hall was beautifully decorated as Katie entered along with the other guests. Three additional chandeliers had been added to the two large ones that had always adorned the long majestic hallway. There were streamers and balloons everywhere and a small orchestra position at the far end opposite the main door. Café tables lined each wall and the long carpet that usually spanned the length of the room had been rolled up to accommodate dancing.

As the guests entered, they gathered along the edges of the walls to await the entrance of the White family.

Within minutes, Ambrose stepped to the middle of the room and, glancing around, announced, "Ladies and Gentlemen, honored guests, Judge White and Miss Margaret White!"

The orchestra struck up a ballad that was unfamiliar to Katie, and the Judge entered the room with Boots on his arm. He smiled warmly at the crowd, but Boots looked like she would faint at any moment. Her father reached over and patted her hand and they made their way to the center of the room.

"Dear friends," Judge White announced. "It is with pleasure that I introduce to society my sweet and charming daughter, Margaret. She is our youngest, and last child, and her mother and I are delighted that we won't ever have to go through another celebration like this one again!"

Here the crowd laughed and nodded their heads.

"What I mean to say is," he corrected himself. "We are delighted that we have succeeded in raising such wonderful children and that, with Margaret, they have all reached adulthood. They can now look forward to marrying and rearing their own children."

"Here, here!" yelled several guests, many raising their glasses.

"So, enough now on hearing me ramble. It's time to start the dancing," said the Judge, looking around expectantly. "Boots, dear, who is your escort for the evening that will lead us off?"

Boots blushed in embarrassment, as she had obviously failed to bring one who, by tradition, would have escorted her onto the dance floor to open the party.

Suddenly a voice rang out. "That would be me, sir!" and Jim Fielding stepped out from the crowd and walked across the dance floor. He approached Boots who was still standing next to her father and held out his arm to escort her to the middle of the hall. Although still blushing, she looked at him with relief and took his arm.

The orchestra began, and Jim swept his young partner into the waltz. Soon the rest of the attendees joined them, and the hall was filled with dancing.

"That was very gallant of Jim Fielding," commented E.M., as he danced with Katie. "And not what one would expect."

"Agreed," mused Katie, looking over her partner's shoulder at Jim and Boots. "It is becoming harder and harder to figure that man out."

"But not an unpleasant project if one was interested in pursuing it," smiled E.M.

CHAPTER 4
THE THEFTS

It was midway through the evening when Christina Clark happened to glance down at her friend's hand.

"Marie," she asked. "Why didn't you wear that beautiful ring of yours this evening? It would have accented your gown beautifully."

Marie first looked up puzzled at Christina and then down at her own hand to discover the ring that usually graced her right ring finger was not there.

"It's gone!" she gasped, holding up her hand. "Oh no!"

"Were you wearing it tonight when you arrived at the party?" asked Christina, glancing around.

"Yes, of course!" exclaimed her friend. "I never take it off!"

"Is something wrong?" asked Ruth White, coming up to the pair.

"Yes," replied Marie, now near tears. "My ring's missing! It was my grandmother's. I always wear it!" she added, holding up her naked hand to show Ruth.

"Perhaps it fell off your finger?" said Ruth, joining Christina in looking around the area where they were standing.

Her spirits rising in hope, Maria joined them and was just peeking under a chair when Katie approached them with a tearful young woman trailing behind her.

"Ruthie," Katie called softly. "May we speak with you for a moment?"

"Yes, of course," replied Ruth, excusing herself to the other girls and stepping off to the side with Katie.

"Ruth, this is Jane Manning," Katie said, placing a hand on Jane's arm. "She's just discovered that her brooch is missing. She definitely had it on about an hour ago and now it's gone."

Ruth gave the girl a dismayed look, her eyes drifting down to the Jane's empty lapel.

"Oh dear!" she muttered to herself. "I don't mean to sound dismissive, Miss Manning, but are you sure you wore it this evening?"

"Yes, absolutely!" replied Jane, the tears starting to stream down her cheeks. "I know this for certain because I was showing it to Mr. Fielding, who told me that his fiancée has one just like it!"

"Fiancée?" Katie said to herself, intrigued by this bit of news but, pushing Jim out of her mind for the moment, asked, "What does the brooch look like?"

"It is circular, with an Onyx stone surrounded by gold leaf," replied Jane, nervously. "It's not very valuable but it is one of my favorite pieces of jewelry. I will be devastated to lose it!"

At that moment, a flash bulb went off, temporarily blinding the three women, followed by the sound of a camera shutter clicking. Those nearby turned to see E.M. popping in another flash bulb and raising his camera to take another shot.

"For the memory album," he announced with a charming smile. "We certainly don't want to miss capturing an occasion such as this!"

"Excellent idea, E.M." sighed Katie. "But we have a bit of a crisis now. Perhaps you could put that blasted thing down and help us?"

"Yes, absolutely!" he replied, placing his camera down alongside a chair and coming forward.

Katie quickly explained the missing brooch. When Ruth added that Maria was missing a ring, both E.M. and Katie looked over at her in alarm.

"This is very unfortunate!" whispered E.M., nervously glancing about. "It means that we have a thief lurking among us!"

Katie's hand involuntarily went to the locket hanging on the necklace around her neck. It was still there.

"What are we going to do, Ruthie?" asked Katie. "I'm sure you don't want to call the police, especially during Boots' debutant party, but sooner or later someone is going to raise the alarm!"

Ruth White bit her lip and glanced around. The orchestra was excellent, the guests were dancing, and the champagne was flowing. They were all enjoying themselves, especially her young sister who seldom found anything enjoyable these days. The idea that someone was moving through the party stealing jewelry right from under their eyes was beyond comprehension and the only plausible thing to do was call the police. But the family could ill afford the scandal, especially since her father was the judge of Fairfield.

"Let's talk to Poppy," Ruth suggested. "Perhaps he'll have some idea as to what to do."

"I'm afraid we'll have to call the police," said Judge White reluctantly, a few minutes later, after hearing what had happened. "I don't like it but it's the right thing to do and I don't see that we have another option. I hate to think what the newspapers will say!"

"Wait a minute," said Katie suddenly, as if thinking out loud. "Maybe we do have another option!"

"Oh Katie!" replied Ruth. "Whatever do you mean? What other option?"

"Let's do a search of the house," said Katie. "E.M. and I will spread out and do some investigation. Maybe we'll ask Mr. Fielding and Mr. West to assist us. We'll start by questioning the extra staff that you hired for the party."

"I'm not sure this is a good idea," replied the Judge. "Aren't we giving the thief time to get away."

"Not if he or she doesn't suspect that we're on to them," said E.M., starting to like the plan. "After all, there is a room of people just dripping in jewelry and the night is still young. One ring and a brooch doesn't seem enough to risk the possibility of getting caught. If I were a jewelry thief, I'd want to stick around for a little longer and try to increase the value of the heist."

"And besides," added Katie. "We're just delaying for an hour. If we don't find out anything in that time, then we can still notify the police."

Ruthie and her father exchanged looks. The idea was risky but better than having a scandal attached to the family. Poppy finally nodded.

"O.K.," he said, raising his hands. "But remember, if you don't come up with the culprit or jewelry in one hour, then we call in the authorities."

"Agreed!" exclaimed Katie. "In the meantime, I think all the White family members should go about hosting the party as if nothing is amiss."

"Yes," agreed Ruth. "We don't want to alert the thief or worry our guests."

E.M. and Katie returned to the party in search of Jim Fielding and Kenneth West. Ruth and her father waited a few minutes before following them.

Katie spotted Jim as soon as she entered the hall. He was dancing with the same young blond that had been flirting earlier with Ruth's ex, Edward. She brazenly made her way through the dancers and tapped the blond on the shoulder.

"No cutting in, honey," said the blond over her shoulder without letting her gaze leave Jim's face. "Besides, isn't it the man who's supposed to get tapped?"

At that very moment, E.M. tapped Jim on the shoulder. Jim smiled and dropped his arm from around the blond.

"So, since we've both been tapped," he asked with a chuckle. "Who dances with whom?" and he reached out for E.M.

"As delightful as that would be," replied E.M. smiling. "Sadly, I must relinquish the privilege to Katie."

"Ah," grinned Jim, stepping around E.M. to take Katie into his arms. "I think I can live with that."

E.M. moved forward and, giving her a slight bow, took the blond into his arms and skillfully danced her away.

"So, what gives?" asked Jim once he and Katie fell into a foxtrot.

"Why so suspicious?" replied Katie, her eyes twinkling. "Can't I just wish to dance with you, Mr. Fielding?"

"I believe you'd rather walk over hot coals, Miss Porter," answered Jim. "But I'm enjoying this, so I really don't care what your motives are."

They danced for a few more minutes until Katie finally confessed. "O.K., I would like your help. Will you follow me?"

Jim laughed but followed her out of the hall and across to the library. Here Katie explained the thefts and the plan to investigate.

"E.M. will search the hall," she explained. "Perhaps Mr. West will help us and search the kitchen while we question the staff hired for the party."

"Sounds good," replied Jim, concerned and turning to leave the library. "I'll find Kenneth and we'll meet you in the kitchen in five minutes."

They left the library and went their separate ways; Katie to question the staff and Jim to find Kenneth. When Katie arrived in the kitchen, she found the usual chaos that comes with serving a large party. There were piles of empty glasses near the sink and, on the opposite counter, the White's cook, Mildred, placing fancy hors d'oeuvres on several serving trays destined to go out to the main hall. Two waiters were waiting patiently nearby to take them when they were ready.

"May I help you, Miss Katie?" said a somewhat frazzled Mildred, glancing up and spying Katie.

"No, Mildred," replied Katie, stepping to one side to avoid a collision with another waiter who was entering the kitchen with an empty tray held high. "Please don't mind me. I just need to speak to this young man here," she added, signaling to one of the waiters.

The young man, whose name turned out to be Marcus, denied any knowledge of the jewelry, as did the other waiters, whom Katie questioned one-by-one as they came and went from the kitchen.

"I think you're barking up the wrong tree," said Mildred, after Katie questioned her about the movements of the two assistants that had been brought in to help prepare the food for the party. "Debra here, has been called in to help me on several occasions over the years and Kitty there, is her daughter. I can vouch for both."

"Of course," replied Katie. "Who's in charge of the extra help?"

"You mean the wait staff?" asked Mildred, and when Katie nodded, answered, "that would be Mr. Harvey. I believe that he's outside taking a quick break."

"This is frustrating," she said to Jim, who had entered the kitchen moments earlier and was doing a search of the area with Kenneth. "I think I'll step outside and ask Mr. Harvey a few questions."

"I'll join you," replied Jim, taking her by the arm. "Kenneth can finish up inside."

They found Mr. Harvey leaning against the company van, chewing on a toothpick.

"My staff is as honest as the day is long," he said, adamantly. "I check their references thoroughly before I hire them! All my employees must be squeaky clean, because we do a lot of affairs for high class folks such as the Whites."

"Does your company only provide waiters," asked Jim. "Or do you include other types of domestic help."

"We provide cooks, assistant cooks, maids, housekeepers, window washers," Mr. Harvey replied. "Whatever the client needs. Mrs. White only needed extra help serving food, so I only brought Max, Marcus, and Joe. They've been with me for years and are my best men."

"I see," murmured Jim thoughtfully. "And do you usually come along to supervise your staff?"

"No, only for big affairs like this one," he replied, and then added indignantly, "if word ever got out that my staff steals, my reputation would be ruined. Why, I'd be out of business in a flash!"

"We completely understand, Mr. Harvey," replied Katie, earnestly. "We're not accusing anyone of anything yet. We just want to find out where the jewelry may have gone missing. After all, we can't afford a scandal either."

"Well, search all you want!" responded Mr. Harvey, crossing his arms in front of him. "You won't find anything on my people!"

"I've found them!" announced Kenneth, leaning out of the back door. "Look here!"

Katie, Jim, and Mr. Harvey rushed up to Kenneth who had stepped from the door and was holding out his hand. In it were three rings, a wristwatch, a brooch, and two necklaces.

"Where on earth did you find these?" cried Katie, picking up the brooch.

"They were in the kitchen closet, hidden inside a coffee urn," replied Kenneth, smiling. "I found them just as I was about to give up the search."

"How are we ever to discover who put them there?" exclaimed Katie. "Anyone could have done it!"

"Anyone, indeed," said Jim, softly, taking the jewelry from Kenneth. "The next trick will be how to return these to their owners without raising suspicion."

"Let's show them to Ruthie," replied Katie. "A few of these might be her sister's missing pieces."

Ruth White met them in the library, bringing E.M. with her.

"Yes, these two rings and this pearl necklace belong to Boots," she replied, picking up the jewelry with relief. "I recognize them. How very odd!"

"Well, that takes care of three of the pieces," said E.M., peering over Ruth's shoulder.

"Oh dear!" gasped Ruth. "This is mother's wristwatch!"

"Are you sure?" asked Katie, taking the watch from her.

"Yes," Ruth replied. "It has an inscription on the back. Poppy gave it to her for their tenth wedding anniversary!"

"To my darling, Mary," Katie read aloud from the back of the watch. "From your loving husband. July 1st, 1917."

"O.K., so the watch can be returned to your mother's bedroom without her ever knowing that it was missing," said Jim, rubbing his chin. "And the rings and necklace can go back to Boots. How about the other pieces?"

"I can 'find' the ring under a chair for Marie," said E.M. "And return it to her. Hopefully it's hers," he added, sighing.

"And I'll drop the brooch into one of Jane's pockets," replied Katie. "And then suggest that she look there to find it."

"That leaves me with the necklace," said Jim, taking it from Ruth's hand. "I'll circulate through the hall and see if I can find its owner."

"And then what?" asked Katie.

"I'll secretly drop it down her décolletage," he replied, grinning as he turned to leave. "Then I'll offer to help her retrieve it!"

E.M. was smiling but, to her dismay, Katie felt herself blush. Before she could respond, though, Kenneth shouted after him.

"Be careful what you wish for, Jim," he said chuckling. "The necklace could belong to Mrs. Horton."

Mrs. Horton was over eighty years old and was attending the debutant party as the chaperone for two young great nieces, Meredith and Constance Fleming, who were classmates of Boots.

"I've found it," exclaimed E.M. moments later, working his way over to Marie. "It was under the tea cart over on the opposite end of the room. It must have dropped off your finger and then kicked along by every dancing couple that unknowingly encountered it!"

"Oh my," cried Marie in relief and taking the ring from his hand. "How ever did you find it?"

"Well, I had just finished dancing with that wonderful young lady over there when I caught a glimpse of something shinning," he explained. "And, *voila*! There it was! I hope it hasn't been damaged."

"No, it looks perfectly fine," Marie replied, examining the ring before sliding it onto her finger. "How will I ever be able to thank you, sir?"

"No need, my dear," he responded, and tipping a nonexistent hat, turned to go. "I'm delighted that I could be of some service."

Meanwhile, Katie had managed to slip the brooch into a pocket of Jane's gown as she brushed passed her. She continued on and then waited several minutes before turning back and approaching the young woman again.

"Dear Jane," she began. "I'm terribly sorry but I have been unable to locate your lovely brooch. Have you looked everywhere for it?"

"Yes, Miss Porter," responded Jane, tears threatening to reappear. "I have."

"Most unfortunate," said Katie, pretending to contemplate the situation. She slid her hands into her own pockets and then, as if the idea had suddenly come to her, looked over at Jane's pockets. "You don't think…" she began. "No… it would be too wonderful…but you did say you checked everywhere?"

"Miss Porter?" asked Jane, wondering what Katie could possibly be talking about.

"Have you checked your pockets?" Katie asked. "Could the brooch have come loose and slid down into one of them?"

"No, I don't believe so," replied Jane, but she moved her hands to her pockets. "Oh!" she cried, pulling out the brooch. "Here it is! You were right, Miss Porter! How smart of you!" she added in relief.

"It was just a lucky guess," Katie said, patting the girl's hand. "I'm just delighted that it's been found."

A moment later, she heard a voice coming from across the noisy hall.

"Young man!" Mrs. Horton could be heard yelling. "What do you think you are doing!"

CHAPTER 5
INCRIMINATING PHOTOGRAPHS

The sound of the typewriter could be heard flowing from the library out into the hallway of the Rosegate Estate as Katie tapped out her article.

"Don't you think describing Boots' party as the most elegant affair of the past year is a bit over the top?" asked Ruth, who was lounging on a couch nearby, the first few pages in her hand.

"No, not over the top," murmured Katie, stopping to glance over the page currently in the typewriter. "Maybe slightly embellished. But we'll see what E.M. says."

"What time do you expect him?" asked Ruth. "Is he having lunch with us?"

"Yes," replied Katie. "And I asked him to bring the pictures he took of the party with him. He should be here any minute."

Ruth got up and, stretching, gazed over at a beautiful bouquet of yellow roses arranged in a vase and placed in the center of a table by the window.

"That's quite a beautiful bouquet," said Ruth. "For your birthday?"

"Yes," replied Katie, somewhat distracted. "They arrived early this morning."

Ruth walked over and picked up the card. "To my lovely dance partner. Happy Birthday and best wishes," she read out loud. "And it's signed, 'Jim Fielding.' It looks like you have an admirer Katie!"

"Don't be daft, Ruthie dear," remarked Katie, looking over at her friend. "He just sent the flowers to tease me."

"Really?" Ruth replied, smiling at Katie. "It seems a very strange way to tease someone. They're absolutely lovely. I wonder how he knew about your birthday?"

"E.M. must have told him," replied Katie, glancing over at the roses. "I agree they're beautiful, which is why I haven't thrown them away He *is* a very strange man, don't you think?"

"No, I think he's adorable," said Ruth, chuckling. "And a bit smitten with you."

"Your brain must be muddled from the party last night," replied Katie, standing and whipping the last page of her article from the typewriter. She walked over and handed it to Ruth. "Besides, I was told that he has a fiancée.

Before Ruth could reply, they heard E.M. coming down the hall following on the heels of the Porter's butler, Andrews.

"Mr. Butler," announced Andrews, stepping through the library door and moving to the side to permit E.M. to enter.

"Ladies!" E.M. exclaimed, stepping forward to clasp Katie's hand first and then Ruth's.

"E.M.!" cried Katie. "I'm so glad you could come! Did you bring the photographs?"

"Yes, dear Katie," he replied, flopping down in a nearby chair. "But pleasure before business," he added, reaching into the pocket of his jacket. "It is unhealthy for you to work on your birthday!" He handed her a small box, wrapped in silver paper.

"E.M." Katie exclaimed. "What's this?"

"A birthday present, silly," he chuckled. "From your new old friend."

"You didn't have to buy me a birthday present," Katie replied, smiling shyly. She carefully opened the box and lifted out a beautiful pair of earrings. "Oh my!" she gasped. "E.M., they're beautiful! Thank you!" and she leaned over and gave him a hug.

"Happy Birthday, Katie," he responded. "And many more! Oh, I almost forgot!" and he reached in a second pocket and pulled out an envelope. Inside was a card.

"What's this?" asked Katie. "A birthday card?"

"A birthday card and thank you card combined," replied E.M. "From Midge Pennington."

Katie looked puzzled as she pulled the card from the envelope. She read it silently and then smiled. "Along with wishing me a happy birthday, she's thanking me for the wonderful time she had this weekend at our cross-country equestrian race. She says she's writing a very nice article for the *Gazette* and that she actually won the competition!"

"You really made her day," said E.M. "When I stopped by the newspaper this morning to pick up the pictures, Midge was working on the article and had the trophy placed on the corner of her desk. It's a real beauty and she's very proud of it!"

For the next hour, the three of them worked on the debutante article and chose the pictures that would accompany it.

"We should add Ruth to the byline," joked E.M. to Katie. "Since she's helped write it!"

"Don't you dare!" replied Ruth, chuckling. "Mother is miffed enough about the newspaper story as it is, without seeing my name attached to it. However, she and Poppy are extremely grateful to Katie for her handling of the missing jewelry. That's the only reason they're letting the article be published."

"I wonder how Mr. Fielding is doing." E.M. mused. "Young Meredith really gave him a wallop!"

"Not to mention Mrs. Horton striking him with her cane!" laughed Ruth.

"I'm just glad that it all got straightened out before she insisted that we have him arrested," Katie said, smiling.

"These photographs are really very good," said Katie to E.M. when they returned to the article. "It's hard to decide which ones to choose for the story."

"Thank you," replied E.M. "I do try my best."

At that moment luncheon was announced and the three friends left the library to join Katie's grandmother in the dining room.

Mrs. Agatha Fitzgerald Maine Porter, at first glance, looked to be a formidable woman. In her seventies, she was attractive and must have been quite a beauty in her youth. She was thin with steely gray eyes and a firm mouth. However, if one looked closely, they would see a perpetual twinkle in her eyes that revealed her true nature. She was a kind and gentle woman who had taken on the task of raising her granddaughter, becoming the only constant in Katie's life. Katie absolutely adored her.

"Gran," exclaimed Katie, leaning over and giving her grandmother a hug. "This is my friend E.M. Butler. E.M., this is my grandmother."

"A pleasure to meet you, ma'am," replied E.M. respectfully. "Thank you so much for allowing me to dine with you in celebration of Katie's birthday."

"Nice to meet you, Mr. Butler," replied Mrs. Porter. "We are delighted that you could join us."

"Hello, Mrs. Porter," said Ruth, greeting Katie's grandmother with a hug. "It's perfect weather for Katie's special day, don't you think?"

"Yes, Ruthie, dear," agreed Mrs. Porter. "And I must say that you are looking very well today."

"Thank you, ma'am," replied Ruth, taking a seat next to Katie while E.M. sat across the table.

The lunchtime birthday celebration was filled with stories and laughter and E.M. quickly felt at ease, despite the unfamiliar opulence surrounding him. Where the White's residence of Sunset Hill was large and lavish, Rosegate Estate, although larger, was stately, elegant, warm, and welcoming.

There was an unrushed ambience about the place and E.M. could imagine how wonderful it must have been to grow up there.

"Look at the beautiful earrings that E.M. gave me," exclaimed Katie, sliding the box over to Mrs. Porter. "And Ruthie gave me a wonderful pair of leather driving gloves. I have been absolutely spoiled!"

"Well one should be on their birthday!" replied her grandmother. "I believe then, that it is time for me to present you with my gift."

"Oh, Gran," cried Katie. "You shouldn't have gotten me anything! You've given me so much already!"

"Nonsense!" replied Mrs. Porter smiling and she rang the bell beside her plate. "Andrews, bring me Miss Katie's birthday gift," she instructed the butler.

"Yes madam," replied Andrews, bowing slightly before disappearing from the room and returning moments later with a small box on a tray. He held the tray out to Mrs. Porter who took the box and handed it to Katie.

"Happy twenty-first birthday, dear Granddaughter," smiled Mrs. Porter. "I love you very much."

Katie tearfully smiled at her grandmother and then opened the box. She gasped, disbelief washing over her face, before holding it up so that her friends could see what lay inside. It was a beautiful necklace adorned with diamonds and alternating blue sapphires and rubies.

"It must be worth millions!" thought E.M. to himself.

"It's beautiful!" gasped Ruth, gazing at the precious gems surrounding the necklace.

"Oh, Gran!" was all Katie could say before jumping to her feet and throwing her arms around Mrs. Porter. "But it's too much!"

"Nonsense!" replied her grandmother, chuckling. "You're a grown woman now and it's time that you have it. It once belonged to my mother, and she passed it down to me. Now I am passing it down to you."

"It's so beautiful!" said Katie with tears in her eyes. "I shall cherish it always."

After lunch, E.M. announced that he would have to be getting back to town. "I need to get this article to Mr. Connors at the *Gazette*. But first, I think I'll fluff it up a bit. Nothing too dramatic, of course!" he added.

"Do you think that it's good enough to add my name to the byline?" asked Katie with concern. "Or do you think you'll have to do a complete re-write?"

"Rewrite? Add your name?" replied a confused E.M. "My dear friend, it is I who is asking to add my name to *your* byline! You've done an excellent job. I just took a few photographs and tried to stay out of your way!"

"That's not quite true, E.M.," Katie responded. "I think that it has truly been a team effort! So, let's share the byline and let the chips fall where they may!"

Chuckling, E.M. took the article from Katie and tucked the pages into his pocket. He drew out the two pictures that they had selected to accompany the story and then handed Ruth the stack of remaining photos.

"For the family album," he explained with a smile.

Putting on his coat and hat as he walked out the front door, he turned and added, "Thank you so much for including me in your luncheon celebration! I had a delightful time! Happy Birthday, Katie!" and he jumped into his car and was gone.

Closing the front door behind them, Katie and Ruth returned to the library and sat down on the couch. Ruth flipped through the photographs.

"These are really very good," said Ruth. "I'm glad that everyone had a good time."

"Yes, indeed," replied Katie. "It was a smashing good party," she added, glancing at the photos as Ruth handed them to her. Suddenly she paused and looked down, comparing one photo to another. "This is very strange," she declared, almost to herself.

"What is?" asked Ruth, glancing over.

"Kenneth West seems to be in nearly all of these," observed Katie, spreading the photos out across the coffee table in front of them.

"I'm sure it's just a coincidence," replied Ruth, vaguely. "E.M. might have been right behind Mr. West as he moved through the crowd and the poor man was accidently caught by E.M.'s camera."

Katie studied the photographs for several minutes before commenting.

"But look at what he's doing when the camera caught him," Katie finally said, pointing to one of the photos.

"He appears to be looking at Meredith Abrams," replied Ruth, looking up at Katie. "What's so interesting about that?"

"Look closer, Ruthie," said Katie. "It's not Meredith he's gazing at."

Ruth bent over the photograph again and studied it for a few minutes. "No, wait," she said, straightening slightly, looking over at Katie. "It looks as though he's looking at Meredith's neck and not her face."

"Her necklace, to be exact," replied Katie.

"Yes, I believe you are right," Ruth agreed. "But what's so strange about that. Perhaps he's admiring it. It was very pretty."

"Yes, indeed," replied Katie. "Pretty enough to be stolen."

"Oh dear!" cried Ruth, finally realizing what Katie was trying to say. "Now I remember! It was Meredith's necklace that was recovered with the rest of the jewelry last night! But surely you don't think that Mr. West was the one who stole it. After all, he was the one who found the pieces so that we could return them."

"An interesting fact, in and of itself," countered Katie, smiling.

"I'm not sure I agree with you, Katie," replied Ruth. "Might you be a little biased against Mr. West since you seem to favor Mr. Fielding better?"

"Jim Fielding has nothing to do with this!" replied Katie, a little too harshly. She took a breath and then added, more calmly, "besides, I have no particular feelings for one over the other." But she couldn't help but cast a glance at the roses by the window. Ruth followed her gaze but said nothing.

"Look here, Ruthie," continued Katie, returning to the photographs. "Let me show you the others," and she pointed to a second photo. "See, here is Mr. West again. He's bending over Marie Castro's hand. It looks as though he's going to kiss it but, if you look closely, you will see his thumb rests over the ring on her finger."

"Yes, I see," replied Ruthie. "But I don't understand."

"Let me demonstrate," said Katie, turning completely to face her friend. "Hold out your hand as though we're being introduced."

Ruth held out her hand to Katie who took it in hers. She bent slightly forward, over it, as though she was about to kiss it and rested her thumb on Ruth's engagement ring. She then straightened up, gracefully sliding her hand from Ruth's, allowing her thumb and index finger to gently slide the ring from Ruth's outstretched hand.

"If the ring is loose enough," Katie began, holding up the engagement ring. "It can be slid off the finger without much notice. If the thief is very good, that is."

"Oh my!" said her stunned friend, looking from her ring in Katie's hand and then down to her naked ring finger. "That explains the ring," she finally said. "But what about the necklace? In the picture, he's just looking at it."

"A necklace is the easiest to steal," replied Katie. "One just needs to reach the clasp and undo it which could be accomplished while dancing."

Ruth did not reply but sat thinking over the situation. It was certainly possible as there had been plenty of dancing and distraction throughout the evening.

"There's one piece that I can't figure out," pondered Katie. "And that's how he got the brooch from Jane Manning." She flipped through the pictures, stopping at one that showed Kenneth West looking down at the ground in front of Miss Manning. Apparently E.M. had snapped the camera's shutter just as something was in the process of occurring because the young woman had her hands up in front of her, a surprised expression on her face. When she and Ruth looked closer, they could see that the brooch was still on Jane Manning's lapel.

"It looks as though something has startled them," observed Ruth. "But there's simply no way to know what it was."

"Quite right," agreed Katie. "Perhaps E.M. knows. I'll ask him when I see him at the newspaper tomorrow. But whether he can tell us anything or not, I have a very strong suspicion that Mr. West is our jewel thief!"

"This still doesn't explain why he handed the jewelry over once he found it," said Ruth, grimly.

"I don't think that he actually 'found it' at all," Katie replied. "It would have been very easy to reach into his own pocket to return the jewelry and say that he discovered them in the coffee urn. After all, no one witnessed his finding anything. Mr. Fielding and I were outside talking to Mr. Harvey."

"Yes, that's right!" said Ruth, thoughtfully. "I remember you telling me. It's all very strange. Why return the pieces once he had taken them? He took an awful risk."

"I agree," replied Katie, nodding. "Perhaps he was afraid that we would call the police and he would be searched. Or, there may be another reason and he realized that he didn't need the jewelry after all."

"Well, I suppose he could have meant it as a joke," said Ruth, getting up from the couch. "But everything's been returned, so there's no harm done. And both Mr. West and Mr. Fielding have left Sunset Hill. So, I guess we'll never find out the reasons why," she added with a sigh.

"I plan to find out, Ruthie," replied Katie with determination. "Something's odd about the whole affair and I'm going to discover what it is!"

"How?" asked Ruth.

"By interrogating Mr. Jim Fielding," she replied, firmly. "I bet he can shed some light on this."

"Do you know how to reach him?" Ruth asked.

"Yes, dear," replied Katie. "If he's where he's supposed to be, I'll be able to reach him at the *Middleton Times*!"

CHAPTER 6
THE NEWSPAPER ARTICLE

"It's not bad, Porter," said Mr. Conner, poking his head out of his office the next morning as Katie entered his reception room at the *Fairfield Gazette.* "In fact, it's very good. It'll be in this evening's edition."

"Thank you, Mr. Connor," replied Katie. "Does this mean…" but the editor closed his door before she could finish. She started forward, but Mrs. Mathers stopped her.

"I wouldn't," said the secretary. "He's in a bad mood this morning. The publisher is after him again."

"After him?" asked Katie, coming to stop in front of Mrs. Mathers' desk. "What do you mean?"

"I mean, if this paper doesn't break a big story soon, we'll all be looking for work elsewhere," replied Mrs. Mathers.

"Gosh, and I've only just started," replied Katie, frowning. "Or I think I've started? That's what I wanted to ask him. My employment here was hanging on whether he liked my story."

"If it's going in the evening edition then I'd say you're hired," said the secretary, and coming from around her desk, she led Katie out into the newsroom. "Let me show you your desk."

Five minutes later, Katie was sitting behind her desk and making a phone call to the *Middleton Times.*

"Mr. James Fielding please," she said into the receiver. "Oh, I see. When do you expect him? No, no message. I'll call again later."

"Hard at work already?" said a voice coming from behind her. Katie turned to see E.M. approaching, a wide grin on his face.

"Good morning!" she said. "Yes, and I think I'm on to something! I don't know what it might be quite yet, but I have a hunch it could be big."

"Can you share what you've got with a fellow reporter?" E.M. asked, perching himself on the edge of her desk, his coat slung over his arm and his hat in his hand.

"Certainly," she replied. "In fact, I need your opinion," she added, pulling the photographs of the party that E.M. had taken and spreading them out on her desk. As she pointed to each photo, she told him of her suspicions. At first E.M. said nothing as he closely studied each picture.

"I'll be right back" he finally said and went over to his desk on the other side of the room. He tossed his hat and coat on his chair, reached into a desk drawer, and returned to Katie with a large magnifying glass.

He pulled up a chair alongside Katie's desk and systematically began to reexamine each photograph through the magnifying glass.

"How strange," he said, thoughtfully. "I didn't notice Mr. West being in so many of the photos but I suppose it's lucky that he is."

"Yes, because you caught him in the act," replied Katie.

"Pardon me, my dear," he countered. "But did we?"

"E.M.!" she replied. "It's right here in black and white! You can see for yourself that he's in the process of stealing the jewelry!"

"But is he?" said E.M., putting down a photograph and the magnifying glass. "Let's look at what we actually have here. This picture shows him gazing at the beautiful neck of an attractive young lady. What red-blooded man wouldn't?"

"But…" Katie started to say.

"And this one," E.M. continued. "It shows Mr. West bending over the hand of Miss Castro's hand. We can see that his thumb is over her ring, but we have no way of knowing whether he slid it off her finger."

Katie felt deflated and her expression showed it. E.M. placed his hand over hers as he continued.

"Finally," he said, gently. "We have no proof, at all, that he took the necklace."

Katie sighed. "You're right, of course," she said, softly. "I suppose I've been foolish."

"Not at all, Katie!" replied E.M. smiling. "I think you have enough to launch an investigation. Most reporters follow leads with less to go on!"

Katie gave him a warm smile and let out a breath she didn't realize she had been holding.

"Thanks, E.M." she said, glancing down at the photographs.

"Now then," he exclaimed, jumping up from the chair. "Before you continue your work on this story, let me introduce you around!"

The next few minutes were occupied by E.M. walking her around the newsroom introducing her to so many people that she couldn't possibly remember all their names.

"Don't worry," he whispered, as if reading her mind. "You'll remember those who count. Ah, and here comes one now!"

Katie looked up to see a pleasant looking woman walking in their direction. She appeared to be in her early thirties, brown haired, thin, and moderately attractive. She walked with a stride indicating confidence and some athleticism. She wore a practical tailored suit and pumps.

"E.M., you impossible man," she said, coming to a stop in front of them. "You've taken my parking spot again."

"A thousand apologies," replied E.M., in a tone that didn't sound like an apology at all. "Please forgive me. May I introduce you to a new member of our little family? Miss Katie Porter, this is Mrs. Midge Pennington. Midge, Miss Katie Porter."

"Ah! Miss Porter!" exclaimed Midge, extending her hand out to shake Katie's. "A real pleasure!"

"The pleasure is mine, Miss…er…Mrs. Pennington," Katie replied, wincing slightly at Midge Pennington's crushing grip.

"Thank you for getting me into the Rosegate Equestrian event," continued Midge. "I had a smashing time and got quite a nice story out of it! Met several nice gals. As a matter of fact, I'm having lunch with Kate and Bet this afternoon," she added, giving E.M. a wink and gentle nudge with her elbow.

"No need to thank me," replied Katie. "I'm just glad that you had a nice time."

Midge Pennington smiled and, giving them a final nod, brushed passed on her way to her desk.

"Kate and Bet?" asked Katie, turning to E.M. who just shrugged his shoulders.

"Let me introduce you to Patrick," he said, gently taking her by the elbow and guiding her forward. "You will want to become his best friend."

"And why is that?" asked Katie.

"Because he is our archivist and can get you all kinds of interesting information from the *Gazette*'s old files."

"Excellent!" exclaimed Katie with excitement. "I have a person about whom I'd like to get more information."

An hour later, Katie was seated behind her desk pouring through a stack of newspaper articles searching for information on Jim Fielding and Kenneth West. She decided to start with what she knew and that was that Jim Fielding told Tom that he had served with Ruddy in Sicily and the invasion of Omaha Beach. However, though there were more than three dozen copies of the *Gazette* featuring, as the lead story, the invasion of Normandy, including the landing on Omaha Beach, she could find nothing specifically about Ruddy, Jim, or Kenneth.

"Well, that's not really surprising," she sighed to herself. "After all, there were tens of thousands of soldiers who took part in the Normandy campaign."

Still, she continued to study each edition, turning and glancing over every page, but finding nothing. After two hours, she reluctantly started gathering the papers to return to Patrick Grant, the newspaper archivist.

"Find what you were looking for?" he asked, as Katie plunked the stack of newspapers on his counter.

"Nope, I'm afraid not," she replied with a sigh. "But I must admit that my search is rather like finding a needle in a haystack."

"Well, let me know if you need anything else," he answered, smiling. "I'm proud to say that the *Fairfield Gazette* covered every major battle of the war."

She thanked him and was just about to turn away when a thought occurred to her.

"Do you have anything on the invasion of Sicily?" she asked, suddenly remembering that Jim had mentioned serving with Ruddy in Sicily as well as Omaha Beach.

"Operation Husky? You bet!" replied Patrick. "How about I bring you everything we've got in about fifteen minutes? It's going to take me that long to pull those copies from our shelves."

Thanking him, Katie returned to her desk and placed a call to the *Middleton Times.* This time Jim Fielding was in.

"Why, Miss Porter!" he exclaimed cheerfully into the phone. "To what do I owe the pleasure?"

"Mr. Fielding," Katie replied, deciding to get right to the point. "I'm chasing a story and wondered if you had time to answer some questions?"

"You're writing an article about me," she heard him chuckle. "How nice!"

"Don't misunderstand me, Mr. Fielding," Katie replied evenly. "I have absolutely no intention of writing an article about you. However, there are a few things I'd like to ask you about concerning Mr. West and his involvement in the jewelry thefts during Boots' debutant party."

"I see," replied Jim Fielding, suddenly lowering his voice to nearly a whisper. "Yes, I suppose it's time I told you a few things. Listen, I'm on my way into a meeting but I can meet you this afternoon. Say two o'clock?"

"Yes, that's fine," responded Katie. "How about at that coffee shop on Elm?"

"Polly's Coffee Shop?" Jim asked.

"Yes, that's the place," replied Katie.

"Good. See you at two," he said quickly, and ended the call.

Just then, she looked up to see Patrick approaching, a stack of newspapers in his arms.

"Here you go, Miss Porter," he said. "Hope this helps!"

"Thank you, Patrick," replied Katie, smiling up at him. "I hope so too!"

Once again, she poured through each edition. At first, she found nothing. However, halfway through the stack, she spied an article that caught her attention. In the July 11th, 1943 evening edition, at the bottom of page four, there was a small article describing the capture of four German spies in the port city of Licata, in Sicily. A team of six American GIs had been selected to sneak into the town, during Operation Husky, with the sole mission of capturing the members of a spy ring known as *"Der Rabe."* It had been rumored that the gang had set up headquarters in one of the small fishing cottages and were telegraphing Allied troop movements and other valuable information to the enemy. The Americans were to come ashore quickly, under the cloak of darkness, catch the spies unawares, and capture them along with their telegraph equipment.

The plan was an apparent success, although there were few details published in the paper. Katie glanced at the photograph that accompanied the article. It showed the four Germans seated in chairs surrounded by the team of American soldiers. Although the faces of the captured Germans were clear, the American's had turned theirs away from the camera, remaining unidentifiable.

"This is no good," sighed Katie, starting to turn the page. Suddenly, however, something caught her eye and she once again studied the picture. One of the GI's had his right hand on his holster, but his left hand was resting on his hip. She could just make out that he was wearing a ring and she thought that it looked familiar.

She stood and, carrying the paper with her, walked over to E.M.'s desk. He was busy tracking down a number in the telephone book, but he looked up and smiled as she approached.

"Find something?" he asked, as she spread the newspaper out on his desk.

"Maybe," Katie replied. "May I borrow your magnifying glass?"

E.M. pulled the glass out a drawer and handed it to her, watching as Katie bent over the picture to focus the magnifying glass on the soldier's hand. Suddenly she gasped.

"What's wrong?" asked E.M. standing up from his chair so that he could get a better look. Katie handed him the magnifying glass and pointed at the picture.

"O.K." he replied, after a few minutes of studying the photo. "It's a group of GIs' surrounding some Germans. What is it that I'm trying to see?"

"Look at the ring finger of that GI standing there," said Katie, softly.

E.M. bent down and studied the GI closer. "Ah," he finally said. "Nice ring. Definitely not a military academy piece but impressive all the same. Why are you so interested in it?"

"E.M., look very closely and tell me if the ring has a coat of arms on it,"

Katie directed, ignoring his question.

"Hum, yes, I see it now," he replied. "It definitely is a coat of arms."

"Describe it please," she urged, resting a hip against his desk and folding her arms across her chest.

"Well, let's see," he said, closing one eye and squinting into the magnifying glass. "It's a dragon with a branch in one claw and a sword in the other. Oh, and there's a motto over its head but I can't make it out."

"*Nescit occasum sol montis*," Katie replied softly. "The sunset knows the hill."

E.M. straightened and looked at her. He said nothing, waiting for her to continue.

"Ruddy," she finally said, looking over at him. "The GI in that picture is Ruddy. I'd recognize that ring anywhere. It's one of a kind."

"Good heavens!" exclaimed E.M. looking back down at the picture. "That's amazing! What are the odds!"

"And now we know that he was involved in a secret mission," continued Katie. "To capture a gang of German spies."

They said nothing for several minutes, digesting the information. Finally, E.M. spoke.

"So, what if he was?" he said, shrugging his shoulders. "What does it mean? Surely, you're not suggesting that this has anything to do with the thwarted thefts of jewelry at Boots' party?"

"I don't know," replied Katie. "But my instincts tell me that they may be connected."

CHAPTER 7
RUDDY'S STORY

It was exactly two o'clock when Katie entered Polly's Coffee Shop and spied Jim Fielding seated at a booth next to a window.

"Right on time," he exclaimed, standing up as she approached and slid into the seat across from him. He returned to his seat and they gave their orders to the waitress.

"I try to be punctual when it means meeting someone to pump them for information," Katie answered when the waitress walked away.

"Getting right to the point, I see," he said, smiling. "No wasting time on small talk, Miss Porter?"

"No," replied Katie. "And I don't imagine you're the type of man to waste time on small talk, either."

Jim Fielding remained silent for a minute and peered out the window with a far-off gaze.

"No," he finally replied softly. "That's one of many things one learns from war." And he turned to look at her with sadness in his eyes. "That time should not be wasted. Every second is precious."

Then the sadness lifted, his expression quickly returning to normal, as the waitress returned with coffee for him and a soda for Katie. Each had also ordered a slice of apple pie, which was placed in front of them.

"So, what's on your mind, Miss Porter?" Jim asked, returning to the business at hand.

"You served with Ruddy White, didn't you?" Katie asked, dropping a straw into her glass.

"Yes," Jim answered, examining the pie with his fork.

"Did you know him well?" pressed Katie, casually. "Were you friends?"

"Yes," replied Jim, giving her a brief look before returning to his pie. "I knew him well and, yes, we were friends. Good friends."

Katie reached for her purse and pulled out the newspaper article with the picture of Ruddy and the captured Germans.

"Mr. Fielding," she continued. "I believe I already know the answer but I need you to confirm something for me," and she held up the newspaper for him to see. "Is this Ruddy?"

Jim Fielding took the paper from her and examined the picture. "Good Lord!" he exclaimed, tilting the page toward the window to get better light. "How on earth did this get into the *Gazette*?"

"I assume we picked it up from the wire service," Katie replied. "Although the story only made it to the bottom of page four."

"So, it's true," he said lightly. "You work for the *Fairfield Gazette*?"

"Yes," she replied, a little more sharply than she intended. "And you're with the *Middleton Times*."

"That makes us competitors!" he joked, chuckling. "How delightful."

Katie chose to ignore his remark. "What can you tell me about this?"

"Well, I'm surprised the story and picture made it into the papers at all," Jim replied, dropping his voice down to a whisper. "It was supposed to be a secret mission, but I guess the brass thought the capture of a few German spies would boost morale. God knows we all needed it," he added grimly.

"Is the soldier in the middle Ruddy?" she asked again, pointing to the picture.

"Yes," Jim replied. "How did you guess?"

"I recognized the ring he's wearing," Katie responded. "It's a family heirloom."

"Yes," he said, suddenly gazing across at her, his eyes twinkling. "Of course! You, of all people, would recognize it, wouldn't you?"

"Well, yes, Mr. Fielding," she replied rather defensively. "I'm a close friend of the White family, after all."

"And you were engaged to marry Ruddy after the war was over," Jim challenged. "But you and he had decided to secretly elope when he was scheduled to be home on leave, just three weeks after this picture was taken."

His words struck Katie as if he had leaned over and smacked her in the face. She sat stunned, her mouth hanging open, her cheeks flushed.

Jim had sought to be flippant and immediately regretted the unintended impact of his words.

"Look here, Miss Porter," he said quickly. "I'm terribly sorry. I didn't mean to sound so callous. Of course, you didn't know that I knew," he added, putting down his fork and reaching his hand out to place it over hers. Before he could do so, however, Katie slid her hand from the table and rested it in her lap.

"Ruddy told me all about you," Jim continued shyly. "In fact, he seldom talked of anything else. He was crazy about you. He carried your picture in his wallet and when things got tough, which was pretty much all the time, he'd take it and hold it to his chest for a few minutes. I once asked him why he did that, and he told me that he was holding you to his heart so that he'd have the courage to go into battle." He paused, remembering the look on his friend's face when he showed him Katie's picture. "I guess that's how we all found the courage to fight. Remembering those we loved back home."

"So, you must have recognized me when you came to Sunset Hill last weekend?" Katie asked, chagrined, but finally finding her words.

"Yes," Jim replied.

"Why didn't you say something?" she asked. "Why act as though you didn't know who I was?"

"I don't know, Miss Porter," Jim answered with a sigh, shrugging his shoulders. "I was surprised to see you there and, I suppose, a little overwhelmed. After all, you had been this beautiful, wonderful, fantasy-like fiancée wrapped up in a wallet size photograph and then, suddenly, there you were, in the flesh, sitting in front of me," he added with a meek smile. "I felt awkward and didn't know what to say."

"Ah," Katie replied, finally comprehending. "You certainly didn't show it. I must have been quite a disappointment after such a buildup by Ruddy."

"No, that's the irony, you see," responded Jim, softly. "You're all he described and more."

"Thank you," was all she could mutter, looking down at her untouched pie and blushing.

They sat in uneasy silence for several minutes before Jim Fielding finally spoke.

"I suppose I ought to tell you about the mission," he said, clearing his throat and spreading his fingers over the newspaper page. "I can't tell you all the details, of course, but I can share some of the background."

Katie nodded. "Yes," she replied, lifting her head to look across at him. "That's one of the things I wanted to ask you about. I'm interested in anything you can tell me."

"Well, let's see," he said, scratching his chin. "I suppose it started when the Allied forces were planning the invasion of Sicily. It later became known as Operation Husky, but we didn't know that at the time. Two days before the date of the attack, Colonel Diggins called a group of us in and told us that the Army had received intelligence that the leader of a dangerous German spy ring, called *Der Rabe*, had set up headquarters in Licata, Sicily. Imagine our luck! Licata was our landing spot. We could capture the spies and liberate Sicily at the same time. He told us that the six of us had been carefully selected to carry out this secret mission. We were to sneak into the port city just minutes before Operation Husky was underway. Our instructions were simple: capture the German spies and their leader without getting caught. Under no circumstances were we to be taken prisoner. If the Italians or Germans saw us, it would have jeopardized the entire invasion operation.

Ruddy, as the senior officer of the group, was put in charge. I must admit it was dangerous and, at times, we were nearly discovered. But in the end, the plan went without a hitch. We snuck into Licata about fifteen minutes ahead of the invasion and caught the ring by surprise. We were able to capture almost all of them."

"Almost all?" said Katie, intrigued.

"Yes, unfortunately *Der Rabe*, the Raven himself, was not there. We later heard that he had somehow got wind of the invasion and fled to Berlin. But, as you can see in the article, our mission was generally a success."

"Why wasn't more written about this?" asked Katie. "It seems like a dangerous mission that ended up being an amazing story. You should have all been given recognition for your heroic actions."

"That's just not how these things work out," Jim chuckled, throwing up his hands.

Katie eyed him suspiciously. "Why do I get the feeling that you're not telling me something?" she said.

"Because, like I said before, there are a few things that I can't tell you," replied Jim, taking a sip of his coffee. "Sorry."

Katie nodded but sat running the story over in her mind. Something was not right. She could feel it.

"Mr. Fielding," she started. "You were one of the six, correct?"

"Yes," he replied, pointing to the soldier standing to the right of Ruddy. "That's me, there."

"How about Mr. West?" she asked, looking closely at the picture.

He smiled and nodded, "Yes, Kenneth was there as well," he replied. "That's him," and he pointed to a soldier standing on the far side of the group, nearly out of frame.

"I'm going to make a guess," Katie said. "And you can confirm or deny it, if you wish."

Jim Fielding chuckled and tilted his head to one side. "Go ahead, give it your best shot."

"I believe that your team was after more than just the German spy ring," she said, evenly. "Something they had of value, other than the telegraph machine, and you didn't find it."

Jim raised his eyebrows but said nothing.

"You and Mr. West decided that, for some reason, it may have ended up at Ruddy's home," Katie added. "Which is why you both appeared at

Sunset Hill."

That got a slight reaction from Jim. His eyebrows had remained raised, but now his jaw tightened.

"Katie...," he began. "Er...Miss Porter... listen to me," he cautioned, glancing around before continuing. "You're playing a dangerous game here, and you are way out of your league. I urge you to stop this, now! I know that you wish to be a legitimate reporter by getting a big scoop, but you don't have any idea what you're up against!"

She had struck a nerve. It appeared that she was on the right track. He was worried. Very worried.

"Mr. Fielding," she replied, as calmly as she could. "I *am* a legitimate reporter, as are you. You are obviously after something big. A story for the *Times*, I imagine. Well, I aim to beat you to it. Besides, I can take care of myself."

She gathered her purse and stood to leave. "Thank you for your time, Mr. Fielding," she said, dropping a five-dollar bill on the table. "This should cover my half of the check." She took a few steps in the direction of the door before looking back and saying, "Oh, and thank you for the lovely roses. That was very thoughtful of you," and then she was gone, leaving Jim Fielding to wonder what on earth had just happened.

As she drove home, Katie mulled over her conversation with him. She was not surprised that her fiancé had been part of a secret mission. Ruddy was a brave and talented officer. But what if the team had really found something of value? Why would Ruddy had sent it home and not handed it over to the proper authorities?

She drove rapidly up the long drive and skidded to a stop near the front door. Once inside, she greeted her grandmother with a quick kiss on the cheek and then headed up to her bedroom to think things over.

She stood in the middle of her room and, clutching the locket around her neck, thought of Ruddy. She had known him all her life and could still easily imagine his handsome face, tall athletic build, blond hair, and his bright blue eyes that twinkled when he looked at her. They had been friends for years and, then, when she was sixteen, and Ruddy two years older, she suddenly realized that she was in love with him and he admitted that he felt the same about her. On her eighteenth birthday they became engaged, just days before he went off to war. Their families were overjoyed and plans began for a big society wedding to be held right after the war ended. But Ruddy was never to return home.

A day didn't go by that she didn't miss him, and the pain of losing him, even after three years, could still bring her to tears. But, as distressing as this might turn out to be, she was determined to solve this strange mystery. If Ruddy had done something he shouldn't have, she was going to find out the truth and make things right, and perhaps even clear his name.

She went to her closet and opened it, reaching up to take down a small shoebox from the top shelf. It had been years since she had read his letters, the effort being too painful after his death. It was still painful but now she approached them with a new goal in mind. Perhaps he had left her a clue in his letters that she had not realized was there before.

She skimmed through the first half dozen, ones that Ruddy wrote when he was first sent to Europe after his training. She could almost hear his sweet baritone voice as he wrote about his feelings of loneliness mixed with false bravado of a quick victory and his return home.

She moved on to the later ones, those written in 1944.

"My darling Katie," began one dated June 4th, *"this letter will have to be brief because we are once again on the move. I have just been assigned to the XXXXXXXX* (here the Navy had blocked out the name with a thick black line) *and will be spending a few days aboard. I have a sense that something big is going to happen but, then again, I have those feelings every day."*

The letter went on with descriptions about the various activities on the ship and of his fellow soldiers. One paragraph suddenly caught her eye. Funny how re-reading the same words under different circumstances could make them leap off the page, when before one hardly noticed them.

"Sometimes it's easy to forget how dangerous the world is around us; we spend so much time marching or lying around waiting for orders. Then a small reminder will come rushing in. Such as yesterday when Jim put on his helmet. We could see the dent in it where a bullet had hit it, nearly flinging the helmet off his head. Imagine if he had not been wearing it! Jim just laughed and said that the Fielding's have always been lucky. But the entire platoon tightened their chin straps after that.

I miss you terribly and a day doesn't go by that I don't think of you. I cannot wait to hold you in my arms again! Remember, as soon as I'm home on leave, we'll get married. Mother and Poppy will most likely be upset at us for eloping and not waiting for the big ceremony, but I'd rather not wait until the war is over to make you my wife!

I love you! Yours always,

Ruddy"

She read the letter twice but could find no hint of a clue. Other than the mention of Jim Fielding, which she had not noticed years before, there was nothing new it could tell her.

As she was folding it to place it back into its envelope, she suddenly noticed a number added to the bottom right hand corner of the first page. She looked closer. Number 44. How strange. The letter, itself, was only two pages long so this couldn't be a page number. She flipped over to the next page and found the number 49 at the bottom corner. Was this some sort of code?

"What on earth was Ruddy trying to tell me?" she murmured to herself. "Are there numbers added to the other letters?"

Quickly examining all of Ruddy's letters, a total of twenty, only one other, the last one he had written, contained numbers on the bottom of each page. He had sent it to her on the day before he was killed, and she had received it three days after she and the White family had been notified of his death. It had taken her three months before she was finally able to open it and read what he had written.

"My darling,

Although it is calm now, I can see dark clouds on the horizon. The battle is getting closer, and we must all prepare ourselves. I imagine that I will be in the thick of it by the time you receive this letter, IF you receive this letter, because everything is very uncertain at this moment.

So, this will have to be short, I'm afraid, and I refuse to waste precious time and words on nonsense. I love you and, no matter what happens, I want you to know that I always will. To my last dying breath.

Katie paused here and took a breath, wiping her eyes free of tears so that she could clearly see the bottom of the page. She found what she was looking for. He had added a pair of numbers on the bottom of each page of the three-page letter. The numbers 55 was on the first, 43 on the second, and 40 on the last.

She placed the two numbered letters side by side and studied them. 44, 49, 55, 43, and 40. What was Ruddy trying to tell her? What did this mean?

Returning to his letter, she read his final words to her. *"The two women I love and admire most in the world are you, my darling Katie, and my sister Ruth."* He wrote, "*I hope you will turn to each other whenever either of you needs help.*"

"I think I'll do just that, Ruddy darling," she said out loud and, leaving her room, went downstairs to telephone her friend.

Ruth was on the other end of the line in a matter of a few minutes.

"You want me to do what?" Ruth White asked her friend over the telephone. "Katie, what's this all about?"

"A mystery," Katie replied, excitedly. "I know this sounds crazy but I'm on to something and I need your help!"

"Well, all right," Ruth hesitantly replied. "What do you need me to do?"

"Did you keep Ruddy's letters?" Katie asked. "The ones he wrote you during the war?"

"Yes, of course," Ruth answered. "Why?"

"I need you to gather them up and bring them over," replied Katie. "As quickly as you can."

"Well, I have to run by the stationary store first but then I'll stop by," said Ruth, and then added, "But I'd sure like to know what you're up to, Katie Porter!"

"If my hunch is right, you'll find out soon enough," replied Katie, hanging up the phone.

By the time Ruth arrived thirty minutes later, Katie was nearly jumping out of her skin.

"It's about time you got here," she scolded her chum. "Did you bring the letters?"

"Yes, they're in this bag," replied Ruth, holding up a gray cloth satchel. "I thought you couldn't read Ruddy's letters anymore?"

"It's still painful but I have made myself do it," admitted her friend. "It's important," and sliding her arm through Ruth's, guided her toward the staircase. "Let's go upstairs to my room and I'll tell you everything."

CHAPTER 8
FOLLOWING THE CLUES

"A spy?" exclaimed Ruth. "Oh, Katie, I simply don't believe it!"

They were seated on the edge of Katie's bed, the stack of letters between them.

"Not a spy, exactly," explained Katie. "More like a soldier on a secret mission to capture one." She then repeated the story that Jim Fielding had told her. Ruth sat in stunned silence.

"The leader of the ring got away," Katie continued. "And I have a feeling that Ruddy was trying to leave us clues in his letters as to his whereabouts or, even more likely, what the U.S. soldiers were really after when they captured the spy ring."

"Mr. Fielding was a member of the team," said Ruth. "Didn't he tell you what they were after?"

"No, he refused," replied Katie. "Apparently it's still a secret."

"Why on earth would Ruddy want to involve us?" remarked Ruth, shaking her head. "I still don't believe he would do such a thing. It could potentially put us in danger!"

"I agree," nodded Katie. "Which must mean that whatever it was they were hoping to get was important enough for Ruddy to enlist the help of the two people he loved the most, you and me."

"I wonder what it could be," Ruth mused. "And who else knows that Ruddy was trying to involve us, which I still don't believe he was, Katie."

"I think that Jim Fielding is beginning to suspect us," answered Katie. "Which is why he told me the story in the first place. He also knows that I suspect things are not as they seem. He tried to warn me off by telling me that I was well out of my league."

"Oh, Katie!" exclaimed Ruth. "He must be right! After all, he knows the entire story and we don't! I say let's leave things alone. After all, the war is over, and no more harm can be done."

"Then why the sudden appearance of Ruddy's mates at Sunset Hill?" Katie challenged her friend. "I don't believe it was because they wanted to attend a debutante party or enjoy a walk around your fountain."

"Well, yes, their timing did seem a bit strange," agreed Ruth, reluctantly. "I have read Ruddy's letters several times over the years but can't say that I saw anything strange in them," she said, looking down at the letters. "Nothing he wrote looked like a clue."

"I thought the same thing myself," replied Katie. "Until I opened mine and found something that I hadn't seen before. Here, let me show you," and she reached over and took the two letters off her bedside table. She opened them and laid them on the bed between her and Ruth.

"Look closely, Ruthie," she pointed. "See, Ruddy placed numbers on the bottom corners of each page of these two letters."

"Yes, I see," said her friend, picking them up to take a closer look. "How strange!"

"My theory is that these numbers represent a code of some kind," explained Katie, thoughtfully. "Perhaps a message. But, since I only have five numbers in all, I may only have half of it. Ruddy may have sent you the other half."

"How do you figure that?" replied Ruth, but she began spreading out her stack of letters over the top of the bed. "It could be a very short message."

"True," nodded Katie. "But something he wrote in his last letter to me got me thinking that he might have split the message between us. I suggest that we look at your last letter first and then work backwards."

They looked at the postmark of each letter and quickly found the last two that Ruth had received from her brother. She opened the envelope of the very last one and, pulling out the letter, gasped. The number 49 could clearly be seen in the bottom corner.

"Just as I suspected," exclaimed Katie. "Quick, let's see the next page!"

Ruth obediently turned to the next page. Sure enough, they found another number. Number 42.

Katie took the letter and laid it down next to the two belonging to her. Then she located the next-to-the-last letter sent to Ruth and started to open it before stopping herself.

"Oh, I beg your pardon," she replied, blushing slightly. She handed the envelope to Ruth. "Would you open it, please?"

Ruth smiled gently and took the letter from Katie. "Not at all," she said, opening the envelope and drawing out the letter. "Although I don't mind you reading it. There's nothing in my letters from Ruddy that you can't see."

"Well, truth be told, Ruthie, I'd be a little embarrassed to show you mine from Ruddy," replied Katie, recalling his letters to her. They were always filled with love and longing.

"Yours would be different, of course," chuckled Ruth. "As they should be. Just as I would be mortified to have you read mine from Robert," and she leaned over to pat Katie's hand. "Now, let's see," she continued, and opened the letter to glance down at the corner. Sure enough, there was the number 53 and on the last page, number 44.

"Katie, look!" she exclaimed to her friend. "You were right! There are numbers in this letter as well! But what does it mean?"

"I'm not quite sure," replied Katie, taking the letter and placing in beside the others. "But only the last two of mine contained numbers. I think we should check the rest of yours, but we can limit our search to the year 1944 when he was in Europe."

They searched through the rest of Ruth's letters but, just as in Katie's case, only the two letters already discovered had numbers.

Katie stood and started pacing her bedroom floor. What did all this mean, and did it have anything to do with Ruddy's secret mission in Licata, Sicily?

Walking to her desk, she pulled out a sheet of stationary and jotted down each number. She was careful to distinguish which numbers appeared in her letters from those in Ruth's.

Her letters contained numbers 44, 49, 55,43, and 40. Ruth's contained numbers 53, 44, 49, and 42.

"If this is a coded message then there must be a sequence to these numbers," mused Katie. "I wonder if Ruddy gave us each a message or is this a single message that he divided between the two of us? And, if the latter's the case, how are we to determine which numbers go first and which last?"

She picked up each envelope and checked the postmark. It appeared that Ruddy wrote to both of them at approximately the same time.

"Well that's no good," sighed Katie, putting the letters down and studying the numbers.

"Oh dear!" exclaimed Ruth, suddenly glancing at her watch. "I must be leaving. Mother will be needing the stationary I bought to write letters right after she wakes from her nap." She stood to leave and started gathering the letters that she had brought. "Will you need to keep those?" she asked Katie, indicating the two letters with the numbers.

"No, you may as well take them," she replied, absently. "I've written down the numbers. I think that's all I need."

"You know, Katie," said Ruth, dropping the remaining letters into her satchel. "Ruddy most likely would have wanted us to crack his code so I don't think he would have made it very hard."

"Are you implying that he wouldn't think us smart enough to break a more sophisticated one?" teased Katie, her eyebrows arching.

"Not at all," replied Ruth, smiling. "At least not where you're concerned."

After Ruth left to return home to Sunset Hill, Katie continued her work on the code. She decided to look for a pattern, starting with how, and in which order, the numbers appeared among the four letters.

Guessing that the earlier of her two letters should perhaps come first, she grouped together numbers 44 and 49. Then, using the numbers on the last letter she received, she grouped 55, 43, and 40. She repeated these same steps with Ruth's numbers so that they emerged as 44, 49 and 55,43,40 and 53,44, and finally, 49, 42.

"I can't make any sense of it," she sighed after an hour. "Perhaps a change of scenery will help to clear my head," and shoving the paper into her pocket, she left her room.

She found her grandmother pruning her rosebushes out in the garden. She was wearing her wide-brimmed "pruning" hat, as she called it, and gardening gloves. A basket lay at her feet for the intended purpose of holding the roses that were being cut but Nugget had found another use for it and was curled up inside, fast asleep.

"Ah, Katie," said Mrs. Porter, looking up as her granddaughter approached. "Would you please remove your Yorkie from my rose basket. He's been under my feet for most of the day."

"Nugget, you silly old thing!" Katie laughed, picking up the little dog. "How about we get out of Gran's way and go for a ride?"

The Terrier's ears perked up and he gave an excited bark.

"It's such a lovely evening that I think I'll go for a spin in the car, Gran," she said to her grandmother. "I won't be long."

"Please don't go far, dear," said Mrs. Porter. "It's nearly 5:30 now and I told Gertie to have dinner ready at seven."

"I'll be back well before that," she promised, turning toward the large garage that housed the Porter's vehicles. "Come on, Nugget!"

Deciding to avoid the route to town, she was soon winding her way along the rural landscape, with Nugget happily beside her in the passenger seat. Katie had put the top down on the MG, and the scarves that both she and Nugget wore around their necks flapped in the wind behind them.

They had travelled only about a mile from Rosegate when Katie spotted a horse walking slowly along the side of the road, led by a man wearing a felt hat, riding boots, and jodhpurs.

Sensing that the rider might need help, she slowed and pulled up alongside him.

"Hello there," she called out. "Are you in need of some assistance?"

"Yes, thank you. I wonder if you could…," he started to say, lifting his head and turning to address Katie. It was Jim Fielding. "Good heavens, Miss Porter, what are you doing here?"

"I could say the same to you, Mr. Fielding," said Katie, startled. "I didn't realize it was you!"

"Ah, good thing for me," replied Jim, breaking out into a wide grin. "Or you might have driven on by!"

Katie recovered herself. "Why Mr. Fielding," she replied, smiling. "It would be unconscionable not to stop and render aid. Even to you."

She carefully pulled the car over to the side of the road in front of Jim and the horse and stepped out of the car. She motioned for Nugget to remain in the passenger seat.

"She's thrown a shoe," said Jim, holding on to the mare's harness and patting her neck, while Katie bent over to examine the horse's legs. "She belongs to a friend of mine and I'm walking her back."

"I recognize this horse," replied Katie, straightening and running her hand along the animal's side. "This is Henry Wilson's mare, Mabel. You're a friend of Henry's?"

"Yes," replied Jim. "He's an old fraternity brother of mine."

"Small world," said Katie, glancing over at Jim. "But look here, his place is over three miles from here! Why don't we take Mabel back to my place and have my stable man put a new shoe on her? I'm only a mile away."

"Gee, that's awfully nice of you, Miss Porter," replied Jim, gratefully. "I wasn't looking forward to the long walk back, nor was Mabel, I imagine."

Katie turned the car around, and they tied the horse to the back of it. Then Jim Fielding slid into the passenger seat, picking up Nugget and placing the dog on his lap.

"Nugget usually doesn't get along with people," said Katie, looking over at the dog sitting contently.

"Oh, he seems fine," replied Jim, smiling down at the terrier and stroking him between his ears. "Perhaps he senses that I'm a dog person."

Katie said nothing and, putting the car into gear, proceeded slowly down the road back to Rosegate. It took them nearly twenty minutes, but they finally arrived at the main entrance of the estate and Katie carefully turned into the long driveway that led to the house. Out of the corner of her eye, she saw Jim Fielding give her a shocked look.

"Is something wrong, Mr. Fielding?" she asked, glancing over at him as they approached the house.

"This is where you live?" Jim asked, taking in his surroundings.

"Yes, of course," replied Katie, giving a few quick taps on the car horn to alert Andrews. "What did you expect?"

"Well, I'm not sure. I really never gave it much thought," Jim admitted. "The way Ruddy used to talk, I guess I assumed that you lived at Sunset Hill with the White family."

Katie pulled the MG, with horse still in tow, up to the front of the house and stopped. Andrews came rushing outside as she and Jim, with Nugget in his arms, stepped from the car.

"Andrews, please ring the stables and get Robert to tend to Mr. Fielding's horse. She's lost a shoe," said Katie, motioning for Jim to follow her into the house.

"Yes, Miss," replied Andrews, turning to follow them. Once inside, Jim put Nugget down on the floor and the little dog scampered away.

"I understand," said Katie, picking up the conversation again, while depositing her scarf and driving gloves on a side table and reaching to take Jim's hat. "I did spend quite a lot of time at Sunset Hill and they have always treated me like part of the family. But Rosegate is my home. I was born here and have grown up here," she said, smiling.

She placed his hat next to her things and added, "you must be terribly hot and thirsty. Let me get you something to drink. I'd also like to introduce you to my grandmother."

Jim Fielding said nothing but followed her down the hallway and out into the sunroom. "Please sit down. I'll ask Gertie to bring us some lemonade." And, with that, Katie disappeared in the direction of the kitchen.

Jim sat down in the nearest seat and took a breath. "What a place!" he whistled to himself and then, noticing the rose garden just outside of the sunroom glass doors, he stood and walked out into it. "And what beautiful roses!" he said out loud, leaning down to examine a nearby bush.

"Do you like roses, sir?" came a voice from inside the doors of the sunroom. Jim looked up to see an elderly lady walking towards him.

"Yes, ma'am," he answered, politely. "And these are very impressive. One seldom sees a Fritz Nobis of this quality. But then, the newer breeds haven't had a chance to fully develop, I suppose."

"Quite so, young man," replied the lady, stepping out into the garden. "My personal favorite is the *La Ville de Bruxelles*," pointing over to the bush, "which goes back to 1837. Quite an ancient rose. Do you have a favorite?"

"Yes," replied Jim, smiling. "I've always loved the Madame Knorr, 1855, but I've been growing the New Dawn. It's only been around since 1930 but I'm having great luck with it. Perhaps in another five years or so, if I'm lucky, I'll enter it into the Fairfield Rose Show competition."

"Well, then," replied the lady, a twinkle in her eye. "I'll make sure not to include any New Dawn in my collection. I wouldn't want to compete with you at the show."

Before Jim could respond, Katie came through the sunroom and out into the garden.

"There you are," she said, leaning over to take her grandmother's arm. "I see you've met."

"No, we have not," replied Gran, frowning at her granddaughter. "I found this poor young man in the garden admiring my roses. Apparently, he'd been abandoned to fend for himself."

Katie chuckled and gave her grandmother's arm a gentle squeeze. "Now, Gran," she replied. "You know that's not true. I told this young man to sit down and stay put so that I could get him some cold lemonade. But, as you can see, he has his own mind."

"And very good taste in roses," added Katie's grandmother.

"Gran, may I introduce Mr. James Fielding," Katie said, nodding to Jim. "Mr. Fielding, my grandmother, Mrs. Agatha Porter."

"Mrs. Porter," replied Jim, extending his hand and gently shaking hers. "A pleasure. And please forgive me for taking the liberty of intruding on your garden. I'm afraid I couldn't help myself."

"The pleasure is all mine, Mr. Fielding. Let's return to the sunroom, shall we?" said Mrs. Porter, turning toward the house. "I see Gertie has arrived with the tray."

They settled around a table as Gertie placed a tray with a pitcher of lemonade and three glasses down in front of them. She had also added a plate of homemade cookies.

"Will the gentleman be staying for supper?" asked the housekeeper, looking at Jim.

"No, I've been trouble enough," he said, modestly.

"Oh, please do," said Mrs. Porter. "We'd love having you and it's nearly time anyway."

Jim Fielding shot Katie a glance but, as she didn't appear to mind, he agreed.

"That's very kind of you," he answered. "Then I will. Thank you."

"I rescued Mr. Fielding from the side of the road," Katie said, once Gertie had left the room. "He was riding Mabel and she managed to throw a shoe. He was in the process of walking her home."

"Yes, it was lucky Miss Porter came along when she did," Jim replied. "Mabel and I were getting quite tired and still had miles to go."

Katie's grandmother looked from Katie to Jim and then back to Katie with an expression of shock on her face that said, "we don't pick up strangers from the side of the road." Katie correctly interpreted her grandmother's demeanor.

"I met Mr. Fielding at Boots' debutant bash this past weekend," she hastened to explain. "He was a friend of Ruddy's. They served together in the Army."

"Oh, well then, that explains it," her grandmother responded with relief, and then added, "such a tragedy about Rutherford. I was so looking forward to him joining our little family."

"Yes, a tragedy," nodded Jim, placing his glass down upon the tray.

"May I use your phone? I must call Henry to let him know about Mabel and that we'll be very late riding home."

"Yes, of course," replied Katie. "It's in the hall. But please let Henry know that we'll keep his horse overnight in our stables and bring her over tomorrow morning in our horse trailer. I'll give you a ride home in the car after dinner. It will be too dark to ride back tonight on horseback."

"That's very kind of you," responded Jim with a grateful smile. "Thank you. And I'll let Henry know."

"So, is he really a friend of Rutherford's?" her grandmother asked after Jim had left to make the call.

"He claims to be," replied Katie, softly. "But I think that I shall remain on my guard, just in case."

CHAPTER 9
THE CODE

Mr. Jim Fielding turned out to be a wonderful dinner guest and time passed quickly. He was charming and entertaining, regaling them with funny stories of his various adventures working for the *Middleton Times.*

"Unbeknownst to me," he was saying. "The young female, named Gloria, that I was looking forward to meeting because my colleagues told me that she gave great hugs, turned out to be a twelve foot python. She scared the life out of me!"

"Did you get your hug?" asked Katie, with a chuckle.

"Yes," Jim replied, smiling. "And a great article as well!"

"Well, young man," said Mrs. Porter, after they had finished dessert. She pushed her chair back and stood. "I must say goodnight. I'm old and need my sleep. It's been a pleasure having you as our guest tonight. I hope that we'll see you again soon."

"The pleasure was all mine, Mrs. Porter," replied Jim, taking her hand for a moment. "I can't remember when I've had a better dinner and with better dinner companions. Thank you."

"Flatterer," teased Katie's grandmother. "Well, then," she said turning to give Katie a kiss. "Goodnight Katie. Don't stay up too late and be careful driving Mr. Fielding home."

"Yes, Gran," Katie promised. "I will. Sleep well."

They stood and watched Mrs. Porter make her way from the room and then Katie asked if Jim would like to join her in the library for a glass of sherry before he had to return home.

"It will give me an opportunity to tell you what I've discovered concerning the spy ring case," she added.

Jim Fielding hesitated for a moment before replying, "sherry would be nice, thank you." As they walked across the hall to the library, he added, "I'm rather surprised that you'd be sharing anything about the case with me after the tense ending to our meeting this afternoon."

"Yes, well, I'm not really sure that I should," she answered, reaching into her skirt pocket. "In fact, I could be making a big mistake. But for some reason, I feel compelled to share what I've found." She pulled out the paper containing the numbered code and handed it to him.

"What's this?" he asked, as he glanced over the numbers.

Katie poured out two glasses of sherry from the decanter and, handing one to him, replied, "I was hoping that you could tell me."

He took the glass and sat in one of the overstuffed chairs in front of the fireplace, sherry in one hand and the paper with the numbers in the other.

"The first five pairs were written in the bottom corner of the last two letters I received from Ruddy," explained Katie, taking a seat on the couch across from him. "The last pairs were on the last letters he wrote to his sister, Ruth."

"Very interesting," Jim said thoughtfully. "I was afraid he'd do something like this."

"Like what?" replied Katie, and then pausing for a moment. "Isn't it about time you told me what this is all about?"

He shook his head and stared off into space.

"I have a series of numbers that Ruddy sent to me," she continued. "That are meant to tell me something, which I'll figure out sooner or later. But not knowing what I'm getting myself into doesn't allow me an opportunity to protect myself. I can't be on guard for something I don't know is coming."

"You should take my advice and not get involved," he answered emphatically.

"You should be telling that to Ruddy, not me," she countered, somewhat angrily. "Because it looks as though he wanted me to get involved. At least *he* had sense enough to trust me!"

They sat in silence for several minutes, not looking at each other while they sipped their sherry.

"A tragedy," Jim Fielding whispered finally. He looked over at Katie and caught her eye. "I'm not sure I should be telling you this," he began again. "But it should have been me that was killed that day on Omaha Beach."

Katie stared back at him but said nothing.

"I know that doesn't make things better for you, of course," Jim continued. "But perhaps it might make you understand. I was beside Ruddy as we stormed the beach. Halfway up, we were knocked down when a mortar shell fell a few yards in front of us. I got several pieces of shrapnel in my leg. We found ourselves pinned down in the openness of the beach, with no place to hide. There was machine gun fire all around us and, of course, the German's were lobbing shells at us. With my leg injured, I couldn't move, and my fate was pretty much sealed. I was either going to get shot or bleed to death before the medics could reach me. I grabbed Ruddy's sleeve and gave it a yank. 'Get out of here', I yelled at him, 'keep going. There's nothing you can do for me. I'm done. But you've got to keep going'. He wouldn't listen. He wouldn't leave."

Katie looked down at her hands as she imagined the scene. Brave, honorable Ruddy. Of course, he wouldn't leave his friend to die on the beach.

"Ruddy kept looking around hoping to find some cover. Something, anything, to hide behind. He saw several guys laying a few feet from us, obviously dead. He told me that he was going to drag me over to them so that their bodies might protect me. I tried to argue with him, but he got up and stood over me, slinging his rifle onto his shoulder, ready to grab me. A German sniper must have had me in his sites, because Ruddy was shot immediately and he fell on top of me."

Katie gasped but still said nothing.

"He died in my arms, Miss Porter," said Jim. "And his body protected me until medics could reach me. That bullet was for me and Ruddy should be here sitting across from you now. I owe him my life and because of that, I'll tell you everything I know about the spy ring case. But you must swear to never reveal any of this to anyone. Understand?"

Katie nodded and, after finally catching her breath, replied softly, "Yes, I swear."

"Good," said Jim, putting down his sherry glass and leaning forward. "You already know about our capturing the members of the spy ring in Sicily and our failure to get the leader."

Katie nodded.

"Well, as you guessed so brilliantly," he continued. "We were after something very important. Much more important than the spies, themselves, or their leader. The spy ring was in possession of a secret chemical formula that, if used properly, could be the cure for several types of cancer. Imagine how many lives could be saved! Unfortunately, this same formula could also be used to create the main component of a chemical bomb so toxic that it could wipe out over half the population of the earth. This weapon would be one hundred times deadlier than our own atom bomb."

"Oh dear!" cried Katie, jumping up from the couch. "If it landed in the wrong hands…"

"Exactly, Miss Porter," he nodded, finishing her thought.

"So, did you find it?" Katie asked, anxiously.

"Yes, we found it," replied Jim. "It was hidden in a child's doll stashed in a corner. As team leader, Ruddy took control of it. I recommended that he destroy the paper right on the spot by burning it, but he reminded me that his orders were to turn in over to our company commander, Colonel Diggins. Ruddy believed that our government would put the formula to good medical use."

"That's just like Ruddy," sighed Katie. "But I wouldn't trust any government with such a powerful thing."

"I agree totally and told Ruddy that we could tell the Colonel that the German spies had destroyed the formula before we could get it," replied Jim. "But Kenneth sided with Ruddy and there was no time to argue so Ruddy kept it."

"So, if Ruddy turned over the formula to the U.S. government," Katie asked. "Why are we chasing jewel thieves?"

"Because he didn't," answered Jim. "At least I don't think so."

"Why don't you think so?" she asked, pacing back and forth, her hands on her hips.

"Because weeks later, when we got our new orders for Omaha Beach, I asked him about it," replied Jim. "He told me that Colonel Diggins had been killed, and after that, he had decided to hand the formula directly over to the Surgeon General when he got back to the States and that, until then, he had protected the formula as securely as the crown jewels."

"Oh my God!" exclaimed Katie, stopping to stare at Jim. "You think that he may have sent it home for safe keeping? Are the numbers in our letters it?"

"No, I saw the formula and it looks just like you would expect," replied Jim. "With chemical symbols, not numbers. You know, like O2 for oxygen and Ti for Titanium and so forth. I don't know what your numbers are except that Ruddy may have been telling you where he sent the darn thing. A post office box, for instance. Or perhaps at his country club."

"No, that's no good," said Katie, shaking her head. "It's been three years, and someone would have notified the family for payment on the post office box. And Ruthie removed his things from the country club. There was no mail."

"That's just what Kenneth and I found out," Jim admitted. "We came to Fairfield looking for such a post office box and were told that Ruddy never had one. We also went to the country club but it's just as you said, his sister cleaned it out. Then we remembered his remark about the crown jewels. Maybe he hid the formula in some jewelry and sent it home to someone as a gift. That person may not even know what it is they're wearing."

"So, that's why you and Mr. West suddenly appeared at Sunset Hill. You were trying to find any jewelry that might contain the formula!" exclaimed Katie.

"Yes, you clever woman," he chuckled. "Kenneth and I suspected that you were going to be trouble, but we didn't realize just how much!"

Katie wrinkled her nose up at him, then asked, "Why did you wait three years? And why not assume Ruddy had sent it to the Surgeon General instead of home? Wouldn't that have been safer and made more sense?"

"Yes, it would have. And that's why we checked," replied Jim. "But it took me nearly a year to recover once I got out of the hospital and the war lasted another year, if you recall. I couldn't do anything until after I was discharged. I contacted Kenneth and we started asking around, discreetly of course, but no one could tell us anything. I finally tracked down an old friend of mine who happened to work in the Surgeon General's office, and she was able to confirm that Captain Rutherford White had never sent them anything.

"She?" thought Katie, but asked instead, "And when the thefts occurred while you were at Sunset Hill, you realized that someone else, perhaps the leader of the spy ring," she continued, analyzing the situation out loud as she spoke. "Coincidentally, may be on the same track as you and was stealing jewelry in hopes of finding the formula first."

"Yes," was his response. "We realized that could be the case."

She sat back down across from him. "Shouldn't you be asking me about my jewelry?" she asked softly, looking directly into his eyes.

Jim Fielding raised his eyebrows. "Should I?" he asked, shrugging his shoulders. "Did he give you anything?"

"Only a diamond engagement ring," she responded, glancing down at the ringless finger of her left hand. "But that was just before he shipped out. So, no, he never sent me any jewelry. Just post cards and letters."

"Good to know," Jim said, suddenly covering a yawn with his hand.

"I suppose we'll just have to crack the numbers code," she said smiling. "In the meantime, I should drive you back to town."

"Yes," he said, getting up from his chair. "I should be getting back. This entire conversation has worn me out!"

"Mr. Fielding," said Katie, as they entered the hall and retrieved his hat and her gloves. "Thank you for telling me."

"About the formula?" he replied, somewhat puzzled. "I'm still not sure I should have but you won't let the thing go."

"About that, yes," she replied, gazing up at him. "But I was thinking more about what you told me of Ruddy and how he was killed. I never knew what happened. The Army could never tell us. I suppose they didn't really know, with so many casualties on the beach that day. But I always wondered. Thank you."

Jim Fielding just nodded as he placed his hat on his head and followed her out the door to her waiting car. He wasn't sure whether he should have told this beautiful young woman with the sparkling blue eyes what had happened on Omaha Beach. She would by now have been his friend's wife had Ruddy not taken that bullet. But, somewhere deep in the recesses of his soul, he knew that he was glad that she was still single.

CHAPTER 10
KATIE SOLVES THE PUZZLE

"I can't make any sense of these at all," groaned E.M., as he studied the numbers on the paper that Katie had pushed in front of him. "We don't even know in which order they should go."

They were seated at Katie's desk in the *Gazette's* newsroom, her paper with the numbers and a blank notepad between them. The din of clacking typewriters and men's chatter threatened to overtake their ability to concentrate, but the noise also provided them with a screen of protection from being overheard.

"Yes," agreed Katie. "It is quite a puzzle. At first, I assumed that they corresponded with the date that they were mailed to Ruth and me. But Ruddy tended to write and mail all of his letters during slow times between battles so the letters came to us at pretty much the same time."

"Hum, how unfortunate," replied E.M. "But, even with that being so, can we assume that yours begin the sequence?"

"Well, it may be pure vanity," Katie responded with a smile. "But I would like to think that mine were the more important so he would have started the sequence with those that he sent to me."

"Yes, that would make sense," replied E.M., nodding. "So the sequence would be as you have written it, starting with the number 44 and ending with 42."

"Yes," said Katie. "But I don't know where to go from there."

"Must be nice to have time to play with cryptograms while the rest of us have work to do," said a sharp voice behind them.

Katie and E.M. looked up just in time to see Midge Pennington approaching Katie's desk.

"I'll have you know, Miss Sports Page," exclaimed E.M., indignantly, as

Midge continued to saunter past. "That Miss Porter is working on a very important story."

"I'm sure she is," replied Midge with a slight smirk.

"Cryptogram?" said Katie thoughtfully, and then called out to Midge Pennington's disappearing back. "Mrs. Pennington, please wait!"

Midge stopped and paused for a moment before turning around. "Yes?" she asked, standing with her hands on her hips.

"Please, Mrs. Pennington," said Katie. "Would you explain what exactly a cryptogram is and why you think this might be one?"

Midge Pennington's demeanor changed slightly, perhaps remembering the great equestrian weekend that Katie had provided her. She visibly sighed and walked back to E.M. and Katie.

"A cryptogram is a type of puzzle one solves for enjoyment," she explained. "However, they were also used during the war by the military to send encrypted secrets. They can be made up of letters or numbers and to solve them, one must use frequency analysis," she added, looking down at the numbers on Katie's sheet of paper. "This one is very short, so the message should be fairly easy to solve."

"Well, we're obviously not very good puzzle solvers, because we can't make head nor tail out of it," said E.M., somewhat frustrated.

"Frequency analysis?" asked Katie, ignoring E.M. and becoming excited.

"Basically, you're trying to find a pattern so that you can substitute these numbers for letters," replied Midge, pointing down at the paper.

"But there doesn't seem to be a pattern among these numbers," replied Katie. "As you can see."

"That's because you're looking at them as numbers," responded Midge, looking up and into the blank expressions of E.M. and Katie. She sighed and tried again. "Look here," she began. "Try to imagine these numbers as letters. In the English language, one letter words can only be "i" or "a". Double letters in words are usually limited to "oo", "tt", "ll", or "mm". So, I would start by looking at the grouping of these numbers as, perhaps, short words." She looked down again at the numbered sequence and shook her head. "Your difficulty, though, will be finding where it starts," she added.

"Where it starts?" asked Katie, tilting her head to examine the numbers again.

"A person usually writes out the 26 letters of the alphabet and then tries to match the numbers of the puzzle to them. In this case, your number 44 could match "A", the first letter of the English alphabet, or "O" the fifteenth letter. So, the first thing you must determine is which letter of the alphabet corresponds to your number 44 and the key to your puzzle will start there. One more thing to consider is if this number really is 44 or two 4's put together? That could make a difference."

"Oh dear," murmured Katie, still gazing down at the paper. "It is confusing but thank you! You've given us a starting point that we didn't have before!"

"Yes, indeed!" cried E.M., chuckling and rubbing his hands together. "You're a doll, Midge! I take back all the ugly things I've ever said about you!"

"Yes, of course you do," replied Midge Pennington dryly. "Until the next time." And with that, she left them to return to her own desk.

Katie picked up a pencil and wrote out the letters of the alphabet A to Z. Then she wrote the numbers 1 through 26 below them. She and E.M. looked over what she had done for several minutes.

"Still doesn't make sense to me," sighed E.M., resting his head in his hands.

"Let's try Mrs. Pennington's advice," suggested Katie, putting the paper with the numbers besides the one with the alphabet. "Let's look at these number's as possible words. What do you see?"

E.M. leaned in to take a closer look. "Well, the numbers that Ruddy placed in your letters could be either two words consisting of two letters or one word consisting of four letters."

"Humm, I don't think it's two words with two letters," she murmured. "Because that would make it three "4's" in a row. The first word would have to have the same double letter and I can't think of any, can you?"

"How about oo oh, or aa ah!" replied E.M. chuckling.

"Only if you're having a tooth pulled," said Katie, giggling. "Or have something in your mouth while you're speaking."

"Well that also rules out the one word with four letters," smiled E.M., pointing to the 4449 grouping. "The same tooth-pulling principle would apply. There is simply no word in the English language that would start with the same three letters."

"Yes, you're right," sighed Katie. "But that returns us to our first problem of two words, with the first having double letters."

They worked for another hour before E.M. threw up his hands and stated that he couldn't concentrate any more.

"I'm hungry," he proclaimed, standing up and placing a hand on his stomach. "One simply cannot work on an empty stomach."

"I anticipated that!" Katie replied. "Ruthie is on her way down to meet us and she's bringing lunch!"

"Really?" exclaimed E.M. "Why Katie, you're a genius!

"Not really," smiled Katie. "I just figured that we would most likely be working right up until lunch time."

It was exactly at that moment that the newsroom broke out into cat calls and whistles.

"Hey gorgeous!" Eddie Hunter, a middle-aged copy boy, called out through the toothpick in his mouth. "Is that for me?"

"Hey there, angel!" hooted Bob Sanders, a married reporter with six kids. "How was heaven when you left it?"

"Be still my heart," muttered Bill Evert, typing through a haze of cigar smoke. "I think I'm in love!"

Ruth White calmly proceeded through the newsroom as if no one else existed and made her way to Katie's desk. She carried a large lunch basket in her arms.

"Interesting place you work in, Katie," said her friend, finally reaching her destination. "How do you put up with it?"

"I just ignore them," smiled Katie. "They're all very silly and, in most cases, not too dangerous."

"Hello Ruth," said E.M., peeking around Katie and gazing over at the lunch basket.

"Hello, E.M," smiled Ruth, giving him a nod. "Shall we take this basket outside and find a nice place to eat? The weather is very pleasant."

"And the air much easier to breath, I'm sure," added E.M., casting a disdainful look around the room at his colleagues.

They spread out a large blanket under one of the oak trees in the park across from the newspaper office. There was a slight breeze that blew through Katie's hair and she reached inside her pocket to bring out a ribbon which she used to tie it back and out of her face.

Ruth had been right about the weather. It was a beautiful day and the three friends dug into the lunch basket with zeal. Soon, the conversation turned to the cryptogram.

"E.M. and I have been trying to solve it all morning," she said to Ruth, as she munched on a chicken salad sandwich. "But we're not having much luck."

"I'm still puzzled as to why my brother sent us the numbers in the first place," mused Ruth. "It's extremely frustrating."

E.M. nodded and then said, "Ruth, I wonder if Katie should ask her new friend, Mr. Fielding, to help us," he teased, glancing over at Katie.

"If you think him so helpful, my dear E.M.," replied Katie with mock sweetness. "Why don't you ask him?"

"Because I believe that you have much more influence over him than I," replied E.M. grinning. "Since you were both friends of Ruddy's."

Katie responded by sticking her tongue out at him.

He responded with a "tisk, tisk" sound and a shake of his head.

Ruth, ignoring both of them, reached into the bottom of the basket and brought out a homemade peach pie. "Mildred's best," she exclaimed. "And I dare anyone to say it isn't!"

"Oh! It looks and smells heavenly!" replied E.M. reaching for the pie and taking a deep sniff.

"Wait until you taste it, E.M.," said Katie, smiling as she reached in the basket for some paper plates and a knife. "You will never want to eat a store-bought pie again!"

"You know, when I was in the army and stationed in Europe, I used to dream of peach pies," he said, dreamily. "You laugh but I'm absolutely serious. There is something very alluring about it and it kept me sane during a number of difficult times."

"Did you see a lot of action oversees, E.M.?" asked Ruth, carefully cutting the pie into six equal pieces.

"A little but I was never in any real danger," he replied, taking the slice she handed him. "I was a war correspondent with the *Stars and Stripes.* But enough about the war," he said suddenly. "Katie is working on a mystery and, as her dear friends, we must help her solve it!"

"Yes, that's true," smiled Ruth, turning to Katie, "Will you show me the code, again? Perhaps I'll be able to see something now that you've put the numbers in sequence."

Katie pulled both the numbers and the alphabet sheet from her purse and handed them to Ruth.

"Here you go," she said. "Look all you want. E.M. and I have nearly gone blind doing so and we haven't worked it out yet."

"Midge thinks it's a cryptogram of sorts," E.M. pointed out. "But, as you can see, we simply can't match our numbers up with any letters."

"Yes, I see what you mean," replied Ruth. "Although it appears to me that the numbers 44 and 49 each signify a letter of one short word. Didn't both appear in a single letter to you, Katie?"

"Yes," answered Katie, leaning toward Ruth to peer over her shoulder. "44 appeared on the first page of the letter and 49 on the second."

"There are a million two letter words," groaned E.M., rolling onto his back and gazing up at the clouds.

They worked on the puzzle for nearly thirty minutes before E.M. announced that he'd wasted enough time on the frustrating thing and really needed to return to work on an article.

"I must get back also," said Katie with a sigh. "I've been assigned to write an article on roses and why the older specimens are better than the newer ones. I'm to interview Gran."

"Well, that sounds lovely, actually," replied Ruth, gathering up the picnic basket and sliding an arm through Katie's. "Perhaps the key to the code will become clearer after you've had something else to think about."

"Perhaps," chuckled Katie, and, after thanking her friend for the wonderful lunch, she returned to her desk to retrieve her notepad before heading home to interview her grandmother.

They spent a relaxing afternoon in Gran's rose garden. Katie had grown up learning about roses from her grandmother but, as she trailed behind the elderly woman, quickly jotting down notes for the *Gazette* article, there were things that she still didn't know. Mrs. Potter had a wealth of knowledge when it came to roses, and many other things for that matter.

After two hours, they retired to the sun porch to enjoy tea and cakes.

"How are things going, Granddaughter?" asked Mrs. Porter, looking intently at Katie.

"With what, Gran?" smiled Katie, taking a sip of her tea.

"With the new job, the new mystery, Ruddy's memory, Mr. Fielding, life in general," said Mrs. Porter. "Pick one."

Katie smiled warmly at her. "I suppose I *have* been running around in circles lately," she replied with a chuckle. "But, believe it or not, all the things that you've just mentioned may end up, to some degree, being connected and will hopefully merge together."

"Now that's a very intriguing theory!" exclaimed her grandmother. "I seem to remember you mentioning a numbers code. Have you've solved it?"

"No, not yet," replied Katie, somewhat dejected. "I'm getting nowhere with it, Gran."

"I'm pretty lucky with puzzles," said Mrs. Porter, "how about letting me look at it?"

"Would you?" replied Katie. "That would be wonderful. I'll run up to my room and get it now."

She returned minutes later and pulled a chair next to her grandmother, handing her the sheets of paper.

"We think it's a cryptogram," Katie told her. "But we can't figure out how the numbers fit."

"Hum, yes I see," admitted Mrs. Porter. "It would be so much easier if the numbers were between 1 and 26, instead of in the 40's and 50's. Then they would correspond with the alphabet."

"Ruthie says that Ruddy would want us to solve it," said Katie. "He would not have made it that difficult."

"Do you have any idea what Ruddy may have been trying to say?" replied her grandmother, glancing at Katie with raised eyebrows. "Perhaps something like 'having a lousy time' or 'put the kettle on'. Anything like that?"

"Jim…Mr. Fielding…believes that he may have sent something back home and wants Ruth and I to know what, or possibly where, it is," Katie replied, resting her chin in her hand.

"Good," said Mrs. Porter. "That's helpful. Let's assume that the first two numbers are letters of a short word. If we are looking for where the object might be located, then I would guess that the first word of your message might be "in" or "on" something."

"Hum, yes," agreed Katie. "That would make sense!"

"It's just a guess, of course," replied her grandmother, smiling. "But we have to start somewhere."

"So, we place the number 44 over the letter 'i'," said Katie, writing the number over the letter.

"And place the next number of the code over the letter 'n'," Mrs. Porter advised, her interest growing. "Just to make sure we're on the right track, starting with 44 on the letter 'i', count to the letter 'n'. Does it come to 49?"

"Yes, Gran!" cried Katie. "I think we're finally on to something!" She quickly filled in the rest of the numbers, counting backwards to 40, being the lowest number in the code and fell on the letter E, to the highest number, 55, which landed on the letter T. Then she carefully substituted each of the number groupings from Ruddy's message to her newly created letter key.

44 = I, 49 = N

55 = T, 43 = H, 40 = E

53 = R, 44 = I, 49 = N, 42 = G

"Gran! I've got it!" she cried. "The message says, "In The Ring"! Jim Fielding was right! Ruddy did send it in a piece of jewelry. Now all we have to do is find out which member of the White family received a ring from Ruddy during the war!"

"Wonderful, my dear!" replied her grandmother, giving her a hug. "There's one thing that puzzles me, though. Why did Ruddy start with the number 44? Does that mean anything to you?"

Katie thought for a moment and then let out a chuckle. "Yes, it does indeed," she replied. "1944 was the year we got engaged. How silly of me not to have figured that out sooner!"

"Not silly at all, Katie," replied Mrs. Porter, quietly. "Because it is also the year Ruddy was killed and none of us thinks about that willingly."

CHAPTER 11
IN THE RING

"Nice work," said Jim Fielding, as he and Katie, once again, sat across from each other at Polly's Coffee Shop. "I don't suppose you'll leave this alone now and let Kenneth and I take it from here?"

"Just when things are getting interesting?" she replied. "Not a chance."

"I was afraid you'd say that," he said, shaking his head. "So, do you think you can get us into Sunset Hill to examine everyone's rings?"

"Yes," she replied with certainty. "With Ruth's help. She already knows about Ruddy's coded message, so she'll understand."

"Wonderful!" exclaimed Jim, smiling. "I like Ruth. She's a peach!"

"She's engaged to be married to a doctor," replied Katie, a little too quickly. "His name is Robert Reed."

Jim Fielding blinked and looked at her for a moment, his head tilted to one side. "How nice for her," he said finally. "Well, see what you can do. Meanwhile, I'll give Kenneth a call."

"Right," replied Katie, wondering why Jim Fielding always seemed to make her feel a little on edge. "I'll call you at the *Times* when I've confirmed things." She grabbed her coat and got ready to leave, reaching into her purse for money to pay her share of the bill.

"Please, Miss Porter," said Jim quickly, holding up his hand. "This time it's on me."

"Why?" countered Katie, indignantly. "Is it because men always feel as though they should pick up the check for us mere women?"

"No, not at all," he replied with a grin. "It's because you never take a bite out of your pie and I end up eating it after you leave. I don't like the idea of you paying to feed me. I do have *some* pride, you know!"

"Oh," Katie responded, wrinkling up her nose at him as she stood to leave. "Well, in that case, yes, you should pay," and she turned quickly and left the coffee shop.

She was correct in her assumption that Ruth would be willing to help. The following afternoon, Katie, Jim Fielding, and Kenneth West were seated around a large table in the library at Sunset Hill. E.M. and Ruth had joined them and, on the table in front of them, were nearly thirty rings owned by various members of the White family. Jim Fielding was using a jeweler's glass to exam each piece before passing them, one at a time, to Kenneth for further examination.

"So far, no good," muttered Jim, passing a beautiful ruby ring belonging to Ruth's grandmother to Kenneth. "Are we quite sure about this ring thing?"

"That's what Ruddy told us in the code," replied Katie. "I'm sure about that."

"What *exactly* are we looking for," asked E.M., taking the ruby ring that Kenneth had passed along to him.

"We're looking to see if there is anything unusual about any of these pieces," Jim answered. "Like a secret compartment or a message etched into the design. Anything like that."

"But surely Ruddy didn't mean for us to search some of these older pieces?" said Ruth. "My grandmother's ring, for instance. Shouldn't we be limiting our search to something that Ruddy sent us during the war?"

"Yes, most likely," agreed Kenneth, examining a silver ring belonging to Ruth herself. "But it's possible that he might have been working on the secret mission before he went off to fight and so part of the clue was already here. He may have waited until the mission to capture the spy ring was over before letting you and Katie know about it."

"There are so many angles to this story," groaned E.M. "It's making my head hurt!"

"Well, then," said Katie, suddenly. "If we're looking at rings that Ruddy left behind, I need to add this one to the pile to be examined." She reached into her purse and brought out a black velvet ring box, placing it in front of Jim.

"I'm sure that won't be necessary," Jim replied softly, looking over at her intently.

"Why not?" Kenneth asked, snatching up the ring box. "All rings need to be checked!" He flipped the box lid open to reveal a beautiful engagement ring. It was exquisite, with a large diamond mounted on a silver Celtic band, surrounded by rubies and emeralds. As Kenneth handed it to Jim, the facets of the diamond caught the sunlight coming through the library windows, sending sparkling rays around the room and across the faces of those at the table.

Looking over at it, Ruth remembered how excited Ruddy had been when he had shown it to her and how wonderful it had looked on Katie's finger.

"Ah, yes," responded Kenneth West. "I remember now. You're the fiancée that Ruddy often talked about. Nice ring."

Katie said nothing as she watched first Jim, and then Kenneth, examine it closely before passing it along to E.M. He, however, quickly returned it to its box and carefully handed it back to her. As he placed it in her palm, he took her hand in both of his and brought it to rest against his heart, holding it there for a moment, looking at her with tears in his eyes. Then he let her go, saying nothing, but his actions spoke volumes.

Katie would always remember that moment, and of his thoughtfulness and compassion.

It took them nearly two more hours to examine all the rings on the table. In the end, they found nothing.

"Well, this was discouraging!" muttered Kenneth, standing to stretch his large frame toward the ceiling. "A complete waste of time."

"Not a complete waste, surely," replied Katie. "We can rule out the family's rings, at least."

"Rings! Rings!" came a screeching voice from overhead. Suddenly a large Macaw swooped down from one of the ceiling rafters above and, with his blue and yellow wings spread wide, landed on Kenneth West's shoulder.

"Aaakkk!" shouted the startled man, jumping a little as the large bird settled on its human perch.

"Mad Uncle Henry!" exclaimed Ruth, coming over to remove the Macaw from Kenneth's shoulder. "Where did you come from?" she asked, reaching out her hand to allow the bird to step onto her fingers.

"Rings, rings," mimicked Mad Uncle Henry, flapping his wings and rocking back and forth.

"These are not for you," said Ruth sternly to the bird.

"Not for you," repeated the bird, then squawked and whistled.

"So, this is Mad Uncle Henry," chuckled E.M., coming to stand near Ruth. "He's a beauty."

"Yes, he is," replied Ruth, gently balancing the Macaw on her extended arm. "He's Ruddy's, or used to be, that is. Ruddy brought him back from boarding school, years ago, after one of his roommates left him behind. Now Tom takes care of him."

"Katie Porter, Katie Porter," squawked the bird, spotting Katie still seated at the table.

"Hello Mad Uncle Henry," she answered, softly. "How's Ruddy's boy?" She stood and held out her arm and the Macaw glided over to her, landing neatly on her forearm.

"He likes you, Katie!" exclaimed E.M., totally enthralled with the lively bird.

"Not really," replied Katie, smiling. "I think he's just used to me."

"Ruddy's boy," replied the bird. "Mad Uncle Henry wants toy. Ruddy toy." Whistle. Chirp.

"How old is he?" asked Jim from the other side of the table.

"The vet says about thirty," replied Ruth. "Which makes him middle age. Macaw's can easily live to be fifty." She walked across the room and opened a desk draw, pulling out a cigar shaped object. She then opened one of the large library windows. Holding up the object she said to the bird, "here you go, Mad Uncle Henry, come get Ruddy's toy. Take it home."

"Toy!" squawked Mad Uncle Henry, and he flew from Katie's arm to the toy, snatching it out of Ruth's hand in midair with his claw, before swooping out of the window toward a large birdhouse mounted on a post midway down the White's back yard.

"Ruddy taught him that trick," said Katie, looking at the departing bird. "He spends all day flying from his birdhouse to the main house and back again. One never knows when or where he'll appear next," she added with a chuckle.

"Ruddy loved that bird," replied Ruth softly. "Over the years, he brought home all kinds of gifts for that silly Macaw. Mad Uncle Henry has a collection of bird toys from all over the world!"

"He must be the envy of every bird in Fairfield," said Kenneth, rather sardonically, as he brushed imaginary bird feathers from his shoulder.

"I thought you liked birds," said Jim to Kenneth, as the two men returned to the table. "At least that's what you told me once."

"Some birds but not all," replied Kenneth, glancing out the window as if expecting the return of Mad Uncle Henry. "I'm not fond of the larger ones. Especially the birds of prey with their large talons. I prefer Doves or even Canaries. When I was a little boy, we had a neighbor who owned a Raven named Oscar. They're very intelligent birds and I taught him several tricks. But I was forbidden to play with him after the neighbor found out that I had taught Oscar to bring me pocket change from the man's nightstand."

That brought a chuckle from everyone in the room.

"Well, I'm afraid I must go," said Jim, glancing at his watch. "I'm behind on an article I'm writing for the *Times*. If I'm not careful my two competitors here might put me out of business," he added, nodding to Katie and E.M.

"We just might," Katie replied smiling. "So, you'd better keep on your toes."

"Always, Miss Porter," he responded seriously. "Always."

* * *

"I've been thinking," said Katie to E.M. as they strolled along a winding path through the grounds of Rosegate later that afternoon. She had slid her arm comfortably through his, their stride matching perfectly.

"Oh, yes?" he replied, stopping to yank a tennis ball from the mouth of Nugget and then tossing it for the little dog to retrieve.

"What if Ruddy didn't actually mean for us to look for an actual ring," she surmised. "Perhaps he was talking about something ring-shaped or with the name 'ring' as part of it?"

"Like a boxing ring," replied E.M., nodding. "Or a 'ring of fire'. And remember, the fountain at Sunset Hill is ring-shaped."

"Which may be why Kenneth West and Jim Fielding were so interested in it," said Katie, thoughtfully.

"So, the fountain at Sunset Hill may warrant further investigation," replied E.M. "Perhaps we should round-up Ruth and Tom tomorrow and take a look for ourselves?"

"Yes, I think that would be wise," Katie agreed. "And bring your camera. I'd like to start documenting our search."

"Ah," chuckled E.M. "For a possible future article, I imagine! Good thinking, esteemed colleague," he added with a bow.

"It's rather selfish of me, I know," replied Katie anxiously. "But Mrs. Mathers told me that the *Gazette* is in financial jeopardy and may go under."

"Really?" replied a surprised E.M. "I've heard the rumors, of course, but haven't wanted to believe them."

"Well, you can get another gig at some other newspaper," observed Katie. "But I haven't established myself quite yet. I need my job at the *Gazette* and a nice juicy story might be enough to keep it afloat and me employed!"

"Spoken like a true reporter!" exclaimed E.M. with a wide grin. "I'd like to stay at the *Gazette* as well. I've kind of gotten used to the place."

They walked along in silence for several minutes before E.M. returned to the subject of Ruddy's code.

"You know, Katie," E.M. continued. "Ruddy may be warning you about the spy ring itself."

"Yes! I hadn't thought of that!" she exclaimed, stopping to turn and look at him. "But why? The spy ring was already captured by the time Ruddy sent us the code."

"But you said that not everyone was captured," reminded E.M. "The ring-leader escaped."

"Yes, that's true," replied Katie, thoughtfully. "And that's another use for the word 'ring'. Do you think he was trying to tell me that the leader is somewhere nearby?"

"Or someone we already know," theorized E.M., throwing the ball for Nugget as he and Katie continued their walk. "Jim Fielding or Kenneth

West, perhaps?"

"Perhaps," replied Katie. "Although I wouldn't think that Jim Fielding would tell me the identity of the team that captured the spies or what Ruddy sent home to Sunset Hill."

"Did he tell you what Ruddy sent?" asked E.M., his eyebrows rising. "Do you know what it is?"

"We're not sure, exactly, but we have a pretty good idea," she replied, giving his arm a little squeeze. "But I can't tell you. I've been sworn to secrecy. I'm sorry."

E.M. just smiled back at her, returning the squeeze. "Well, I shouldn't think it quite matters what it is exactly," he replied with a shrug. "As long as we know that we need to look for 'something' and that it relates to the words 'In the ring.'"

They walked on silently for a while, both deep in thought. Finally, E.M. looked over at his walking partner and said, "Aren't you going to ask me?"

"Ask you what?" Katie replied, glancing over at Nugget who had spotted a squirrel and was chasing after it.

"If I'm *Der Rabe*, the escaped leader of the gang?" replied E.M., smiling but looking intently into her eyes.

"Are you?" asked Katie, looking intently back at him.

"No," E.M. finally answered with a sigh. "Although it would have been rather glamorous if I was. Imagine the thrill of espionage, creating diabolical schemes, meetings in dark alleys, passwords and secret handshakes, the exciting heart-pounding suspense of evading capture!"

"You're a little crazy, you know that friend?" replied Katie, chuckling. She glanced over and shouted at her mischievous little Yorkie. "Nugget come here! Leave that poor creature alone."

"Yes, I suppose I am," smiled E.M. "But seriously, Katie, please be careful," he added, softly. "These days it's hard to know your friends from your enemies."

CHAPTER 12
TOM TAKES A TUMBLE

The next afternoon found Katie, E.M., Ruth, and Tom White searching the old fountain on the back side of the Sunset Hill estate.

E.M. was standing back a few feet, moving slowly around the structure, taking several photographs.

"Ruth, your fountain is truly gorgeous," he exclaimed to Ruth, as he took another shot. "It reminds me of the *Fontaines de la Concorde* in Paris."

"Thank you, E.M.," replied Ruth, straightening up from her search of a low crevice in the rim of the fountain's basin. She leaned over and dipped her hands into the water to wash off some grime. "But the fountain is hardly mine. You have an excellent eye, though. It was commission by our great-great-grandfather and is, indeed, a copy of the one in Paris. Smaller in scale, of course."

"Don't be such a bore, Ruthie," said her younger brother from atop the large fountain. "You might as well say the fountain's yours. It will be when Poppy dies. Along with the main house and the rest of the estate."

Ruth ignored Tom's comments, but Katie looked upward from where she was standing knee deep in the water and shot him a disgusted look.

"Stop being an idiot, Thomas White," she exclaimed. "You know that Ruthie has nothing to do with those decisions. I'd keep my remarks to myself if I were you."

"I didn't say that she did, oh future wife of mine," replied Tom, goading her. "I'm just saying that she should admit to the fact that, as next in line, she inherits the whole empire since Ruddy's gone." He pushed back from his perch, one hand clutching the edge of the fountain while stretching out the other as if to illustrate the expanse of the property.

"Be careful, Tom," cried his sister, but it was too late. Tom lost his grip on the slippery fountain and came plummeting down, landing in the water only three feet from Katie.

Both Ruth and E.M. let out a gasp but Katie, realizing that Tom was not moving, rushed forward, grabbing him by the shirt collar and lifting his head and shoulders out of the water. The young man appeared to be unconscious. She dropped down onto her knees, wrapping her arms around his chest, to keep him from sliding back underneath.

"Call for a doctor," E.M. shouted to Ruth, and she lost no time in rushing back in the direction of the house. Meanwhile, E.M. put down the camera and stepped into the fountain's water basin, carefully making his way toward Katie and Tom.

"I don't think he's breathing," said Katie, her voice muffled against Tom's shoulder. "I can't feel his chest moving."

E.M. bent down and expertly placed two fingers on Tom's neck. "He has no pulse," he declared grimly. "We're going to have to get him on the grass and see if we can resuscitate him."

"I don't think I ..." Katie started to say but before she could finish, E.M. gently lifted Tom into his arms and stepped over the side of the basin. He carefully laid the young man down on his back and straddled his body. Tom's right leg, just above the knee, was bent at an awkward angle.

"I'm going to need your help, Katie," he said, speaking calmly over his shoulder.

Katie immediately stepped out of the basin and knelt beside E.M. and unresponsive Tom.

"We don't have time to check if he's broken his neck," said E.M. and he started pushing up on Tom's lungs. "So, you'll have to take hold of his head with one hand and gently cradle his neck in the other."

Katie moved to the top of Tom's body and slid her hands under his head and neck as E.M. directed.

"If what I'm doing works," continued E.M., "I'm going to have to roll him onto his side. You'll have to cradle his head but let it follow along with his shoulders naturally. Don't try to move it yourself. Do you understand?"

Katie nodded her head. "Yes, I understand," was all she could say as E.M. continued to push up on Tom's lungs, trying to force the water out of his limp body. It seemed like hours had passed but it was less than forty-five seconds when they heard a gurgling sound and then a cough come from deep inside Tom's chest.

"There now," said E.M. almost to himself, as he quickly moved off Tom and gently rolled him onto his side. Katie cradled Tom's head as instructed, guiding it over. Within seconds, water came flowing from Tom's mouth.

"Again," directed E.M. rolling Tom once again onto his back and pushing on his lungs. Katie continued to gently cradle his head and neck.

Another thirty seconds went by and then, suddenly, Tom began to cough and sputter and E.M. and Katie quickly rolled him onto his side again as more water flooded from his mouth. Finally, they heard Tom moan and saw his eyes flutter open.

"He's coming around," said Katie softly, relief evident in her voice.

"Yes, I believe he is," agreed E.M., studying the young man intently. "Let's roll him onto his back."

It was at that moment that they heard the ambulance and looked up to see it driving across the lawn in their direction. It came to an abrupt stop a few feet in front of them, the two medics jumping out of the vehicle and dropping down beside the moaning Tom. E.M. and Katie quickly stood and stepped out of their way.

They stood with Ruth and watched Tom being strapped onto the stretcher and loaded into the ambulance. Quite by accident, Katie discovered that E.M. was shaking. She had reached over to take his hand and felt it trembling.

"Are you alright?" she asked him in a whisper, giving his hand a gentle squeeze.

"Yes, of course," he replied, smiling weakly as he turned to look at her. "It's just post-war jitters, I'm afraid. The doctors tell me it might take several years before I get my nerve back."

"Well, I'd say you've definitely gotten your nerve back," replied Katie. "You really kept a cool head. That was the quickest, smartest, bravest thing I've ever seen. You saved Tom's life!"

"You're being kind, Katie," said E.M., putting up his hand to stop her. "But I just tried something that I'd seen done in the war. Besides, you saved him as well. If you hadn't kept his head and shoulders out of the water, he would have drowned."

"I'd say you both saved him," exclaimed Ruth, stepping forward and wrapping her arms around them both. "And I don't know how I'll ever be able to thank you!"

It was two hours later when Katie received the phone call. After Tom's terrible accident, the search for whatever it was that Ruddy had sent home was called off and Katie and E.M. had left Sunset Hill to return to their homes and change into dry clothing.

Katie's grandmother had been concerned when she saw her granddaughter arrive home soaking wet and disheveled, and she was greatly disturbed to find out the reason why.

"Do you think Tom will be alright?" she had asked, as Katie dried her hair with a towel.

"I hope so, Gran," replied Katie. "It was obvious that his leg was broken but we didn't have the opportunity to assess him for other injuries."

"This is terrible!" exclaimed Mrs. Porter, getting up from her chair and walking to Katie's bedroom door. "But it could have been far worse had you and Mr. Butler not been there. I shall call Mary now to express my sympathy over the accident and inquire about the condition of her son."

So, when Katie heard the phone ring, she had assumed it was for her grandmother who, perhaps, had left a message for Mrs. White and was receiving a return call.

"Hello?" she said into the phone as Andrews handed her the receiver.

"Would you like the article to list you as Miss Katie Porter, or Miss Porter of Rosegate?" asked a familiar sounding voice at the other end of the line.

"Mr. Fielding!" she exclaimed. "What in the world are you talking about?"

"The article that's being written about you for this evening's edition of the *Middleton Times*," replied Jim, teasing. "The one about you and E.M. Butler playing in the fountain at Sunset Hill."

"How in the world did you find out about that?" she replied rather emphatically. "I've only just now dried off!"

"One of our intrepid reporters, Randy Brooks, likes to hang out at the hospital on slow news days to see if any of our famous locals come in seeking medical attention," replied Jim. "Imagine his surprise when young Tom White arrived by ambulance with his father, the Honorable Judge James White, trailing behind in his car."

"You guys are vultures, you know that!" Katie said with some disgust. "It was a very serious accident!"

"Yes, well, even vultures have to make a living," he replied. "Anyway, Judge White spoke to Randy about thirty minutes later and explained what had happened. You and E.M. are local heroes!"

She ignored his last remark and asked, her voice heavy with concern, "did Poppy say anything about Tom's condition? Is he going to be alright?"

"Yes," replied Jim, his voice now serious. "He has a broken right femur, which is bad, and a large knot on the back of his head, which he received when he hit the bottom of the basin and knocked himself unconscious. If you hadn't grabbed him, he most certainly would have drowned."

Katie said nothing for several minutes, shivering slightly over the realization that the Whites came very close to losing yet another one of their sons.

It was Jim who finally spoke. "Tom doesn't remember much about his fall. It was Ruth who told her father what happened so that the Judge could tell the doctors and Randy. Nothing was said about why the four of you were at the fountain. Were you searching it for the formula?"

"Yes," Katie responded softly. "We were. But I only told them that we were searching for clues. I've never told anyone about the formula, not even E.M."

"Good. But why the fountain?" asked Jim.

"E.M. and I wondered if we might have been taking Ruddy's code too literally," she answered, leaning back against the wall. "What if he hadn't actually meant a ring one wears? Maybe he meant something ring-shaped or with the word 'ring' in it. We remembered that you and Mr. West had gone down to the fountain to talk and had circled it several times."

"Ah, yes," recalled Jim. "We were actually looking for a spot in which to speak privately. Kenneth suggested that we examine the fountain to make sure no listening devices had been installed."

"It was a long shot, I admit," said Katie, sighing. "But we had to start somewhere and that seemed as good a place as any."

"Judge White said that Tom was at the very top of the structure and slipped off while showing off for you and E.M." said Jim, softly.

"He slipped off because he was taunting his sister over her inheritance and not paying attention," corrected Katie. "He let go with one of his hands while leaning away from the fountain and that caused him to lose his grasp."

"Is Ruth to inherit quite a lot of money?" asked Jim, with interest. "Is Dr. Robert Reed rich?"

"Ruth will gain an inheritance in her own right," replied Katie sternly. "Which has nothing to do with her marrying Robert. When Ruddy was killed, Ruthie became next in line to inherit the Sunset Hill Estate when Poppy dies."

"Very interesting" Jim mused. "The house, grounds, everything?"

"Yes," answered Katie, and then asked, "why the sudden interest?"

"Well, it's just a theory, mind you," Jim replied hesitantly. "And I hate to even imagine it but what if Ruddy ....no, forget it... he would never do that!"

"Do what?" said Katie, tapping her foot on the floor. "You are a very exasperating man, Mr. Fielding!"

"Alright, but remember, I'm not saying this is what Ruddy did," he began. "It's just a hunch."

"Please, Mr. Fielding," she nearly shouted into the phone. "Out with it. What is your hunch?"

"What if Ruddy sent the formula back to Sunset Hill so that he could sell it to the highest bidder upon his return," said Jim, quickly. "I can imagine that the estate is quite costly to run. Estates that size usually are. Ruddy was proud of Sunset Hill. He wore the family crest on a ring on his finger. It would be very tempting to sell something valuable like the formula and be able to secure the estate for years to come."

"You're crazy," replied Katie, shocked. "Ruddy would never do that. It would be betraying his country. No! The thought would never cross his mind!"

"I'm not suggesting that he would have sold it to an evil government," said Jim. "Or anyone like that. But if he could sell it to the U.S. government or another friendly nation that would use the formula for good purposes, then why not? Ruddy wins and so does the government."

Katie paused for a moment, pondering Jim's theory. Would Ruddy really risk that? Would he sell the formula to the US government instead of just handing it over? No, it wasn't Ruddy's to sell. He would have known that.

"There is one thing wrong with your theory," she said. "Ruddy was a combat soldier. He would not have been certain that he would survive the war and make it home, so why take the risk?"

"That's where my interest in Ruth comes in," Jim countered. "Ruddy must have known that his sister would inherit the estate if he was killed. So, he may have thought it still a good idea to send the formula home. That way, if he didn't make it back, Ruth would have it and, thus, the means to financially secure Sunset Hill for generations of Whites to come."

"Wouldn't he have made sure she knew about it and that it was worth a lot of money?" argued Katie. "All we have is a code that alludes to its location, and we're not even sure about that."

"Yes, that's true," replied Jim, thoughtfully. "As I said, this is only one theory."

They were silent for a moment, both deep in thought. Finally, Katie spoke.

"I don't believe that either Ruddy or Ruth would ever sell the formula for money, regardless of how much it might be needed," she said, evenly. "And I'm not sure it *IS* needed. I believe that the estate does quite well through the renting of its extensive farmland and the granting of grazing rights."

"You're probably right, of course, Miss Porter," replied Jim, sighing. "After all, you know the parties involved much better than I. But I sure wish Ruddy had left behind a journal or even a note that would have given us an idea as to what was in his mind."

"So do I, Mr. Fielding," she agreed. "So do I."

Very early the following morning, Katie drove to the hospital to visit Tom. Although visiting hours had only just begun, she found Ruth and Mrs. White already by Tom's bedside. Mrs. White was asleep in a large chair, but Ruth jumped up to greet her.

"We've been here all night," she whispered, taking Katie's elbow and guiding her over to the corner of the room. "Mother didn't want to leave him, so I stayed as well."

"You look exhausted, Ruthie," said Katie quietly, reaching over and taking her hand. "How is he doing?" she asked, looking back at the sleeping patient.

"He's a bit banged up," replied her friend. "But things could have been far worse. What's a broken leg when it could have been a loss of life?"

Katie took a deep breath and nodded. "I can't think about it without shaking," she admitted.

"Yes, I know what you mean," agreed Ruth. "Perhaps this will convince Tom to act his age, but I honestly don't believe it. He's such a show-off, especially if you're around, Katie."

"Oh, surely not!" replied Katie, surprised. "I'm fond of him, of course, but since Ruddy…"

"I know, Katie," interrupted Ruth, gently. "You don't have to explain things to me. I completely understand."

They turned and watched Tom for a few moments, before Katie found a chair and sat down. Ruth gently woke her mother.

"Why don't you go home, mother," said Ruth. "Katie is here, and Robert says Tom is going to be O.K. I'll stay a while longer."

Mrs. White slowly awoke and gazed up at her daughter as she yawned and gently rubbed her eyes.

"Yes, you're probably right," smiled Mrs. White, and then she sat upright and turned to look at Katie. "Katie, my dear girl, thank you for saving my reckless young son."

"No need to thank me, Mrs. White," replied Katie, smiling back at her. "I'm just glad I was there to help drag him out of that darn fountain!"

"Indeed!" chuckled Mrs. White, with relief. "Well children, I believe I will go home now. I'm rather stiff from sleeping in this extremely uncomfortable chair."

She gathered her coat, hat, and purse before bending over to give Tom a light kiss on the forehead. Then, with a quick wave to Ruth and Katie, she quietly left the room.

"So, Robert is Tom's attending physician?" asked Katie, after a few minutes.

"Yes, we were lucky that he was on duty when Tom was brought in," replied Ruth. "One of the benefits of being engaged to a doctor, I suppose," she added, her eyes twinkling.

"Yes, I can imagine," chuckled Katie. "Especially when one has a brother like yours!"

"I agree," replied Ruth, smiling. "I suppose I'd better hang on to Robert for a while!"

They exchanged smiles and then returned to sitting quietly for several minutes. Katie found herself thinking about the conversation she had with Jim Fielding the night before.

She finally said, "Ruthie, this may sound like a strange question but did the Army ever return Ruddy's things after he was killed?"

"Yes, about two weeks later," replied Ruth. "Don't you remember how terrible it was when the box arrived?"

"No," sighed Katie. "But I was too much in shock to remember much of anything during that time, I'm afraid."

"Yes, that's right," Ruth said, thinking back to those dark days. "I remember asking if you wanted to look through it with us, but you only cried and shook your head. In the end, it was too much for any of us and we had Ambrose take it up to the attic unopened. It should still be there. Why do you ask, Katie?"

"Oh, well...," she replied with a shrug of her shoulders. "Jim Fielding mentioned that it would have been nice if Ruddy had left us a note or journal entry that could help us with this mysterious code situation," she explained.

It seemed strange to be talking about an old code when Ruddy's younger brother lay injured in a hospital bed. But Ruth understood what she meant.

"Yes, I see," she replied, thoughtfully. "That would be helpful. Maybe he did carry a journal and it's with the rest of his personal effects. Why not look? Surely you can face opening the box after three years?"

"I'm not so sure about that, Ruthie," Katie murmured softly. "Yet, if Ruddy has left us a vital clue, it could be the key to the resolution of a very serious situation. I'm not at liberty to give you the details but it is important." She paused to examine the depth of her feelings before finally adding, with a shake of her head, "No, I'm not sure I have the courage to face it."

Ruth White looked at her friend closely. "Well, if it's that important then perhaps now is the time to be brave, Katie Porter."

CHAPTER 13
THE EVIL AMONG US

Katie studied the back of Ambrose's head as she followed him up the staircase to the attic and decided that it had a very nice shape. His receding hairline had left just enough hair to require the use of a comb but not enough to be deemed ostentatious.

"Just the correct look for a butler," she mused. "Which he is, of course. Then again, Andrews also looks like a butler, although he has a nice full head of hair," she added in her mind. "And why on earth am I pondering the heads of butlers? I must be going out of my mind." But Katie knew the truth. She was trying desperately to distract herself from the task ahead.

She had followed Ruth from the hospital to Sunset Hill for lunch and then, with Ruth's encouragement, decided it was time she opened Ruddy's box. It took all she had to move, one step at a time, up to the attic. Ruth had insisted that Ambrose go with her to point out where he had placed the box, but Katie was fairly certain that she would have instinctually found it anyway. She guessed that Ruth was making sure she made it as far as the attic, at least. Whether Katie would make it to Ruddy's box was anyone's guess, including her own.

It lay in a corner near a window, covered in dust with the words, "Judge and Mrs. James White, Sunset Hill, Fairfield" written across the top. Wiping her hand over the taped seal that held it closed, she looked up at Ambrose and, thanking him, told him that she would call if she needed assistance. The butler handed her a knife to cut the tape, and, with a slight bow, gratefully left the room.

Katie held her breath, blinked twice, and then, before she could talk herself out of it, cut the tape and yanked open the lid. The first thing she saw was the jacket of his dress uniform. It was folded neatly so that the upper left side was visible, revealing a row of his war ribbons just above the pocket. As she reached to pull it out of the box, she could see that his captain's bars were still affixed on his epaulettes. She gently lifted it out and held it up in front of her, shocked to find that she could detect Ruddy's scent. The collar still held the faint remnants of his cologne. She'd know it anywhere. It was nearly her undoing, and she quickly placed it to the side and forced herself to continue.

She pulled out two pair of pants, three shirts, three undershirts, four pair of socks, three pair of underwear, and a cap. As she worked her way through the clothing, she patted each pocket for the presence of paper or a small booklet. None was found.

At the bottom of the box was a pair of dress shoes, still neatly shined, and a small cardboard box. She opened the box carefully, puzzled by what she might find. Inside was a stack of letters, neatly tied together with a blue ribbon. She flipped through them, finding the vast majority were from her. He had kept every single one that she had ever sent him. Next, she saw his wallet, which rather surprised her. She had expected that he would have been buried with it still in his fatigues pocket. Someone, perhaps a chaplain, had removed it along with any other personal items so that these could be sent home to his grieving family.

She opened it and immediately saw her picture staring back at her from the clear plastic compartment. She clearly remembered putting on the dress that Ruddy loved best on her and going into town to sit for it, just in time to give it to him before he left. This was the photograph that he had shown Jim Fielding.

She flipped open the long compartment that held money and found that it contained a five dollar bill, and some French currency. There was a slip of paper with the address of an English shop that sold pet items.

"Ruddy and that silly bird," she said, sighing out loud. "I wonder if Mad Uncle Henry received a gift all the way from England."

Placing the wallet next to the stack of letters, she reached in the box to pull out the very last item. And there it was. A journal. With the name "Rutherford White" embossed across the front in gold lettering.

She pulled a chair closer to the window and sat down, opening the journal to the first entry. She felt a pang in her heart as she immediately recognized Ruddy's handwriting sprawled across the page in bold black ink.

The entry was dated just after he finished basic training and was boarding the ship for England.

"It's strange to be excited about going to Europe," he wrote. *"I suppose it's because I know that I'll be participating in something bigger and more important than anything else I've ever done before. I do miss my family, and my darling Katie, but this only makes me more determined to join the fight to keep the world free from tyranny."*

Katie grimaced slightly. She had been against his going, of course, although she realized that he had no choice. In the end, those bent on tyranny were defeated. But so many perished in the war, so many Allied deaths, so many innocent civilian lives lost. Was the world really a safer place? She hoped so because Ruddy gave his life for it and she would never see him again.

The next several entries were stories about his life on the troop ship travelling across the Atlantic Ocean. He wrote of being homesick, of the numerous card games that the men played to pass the time, movies shown on board, and, surprisingly, how he first met Jim Fielding.

"Last night, we were invited to gather on the ship's main deck to listen to a concert put on by several new members of the Marine Corp band. They numbered only about fifteen musicians, but one would never know it because they sounded like a complete orchestra. Major Glenn Miller could not have done better!

Halfway through the concert, they asked one of the Army Lieutenants to come up and sing 'I'll be seeing you', and boy could that guy sing! He brought the house down and we insisted he sing a couple more numbers. Afterwards, I had a chance to talk with him and found out that he's from my part of the country. His name is Jim Fielding and I think we're going to be good friends. I bet my sister Ruth would really like him. I'll introduce them as soon as we get home."

"Well, well," whispered Katie out loud. "What surprising things I'm finding out about you, my dear Mr. Fielding!"

As she turned the pages, she noted that, once he arrived in England, his entries started to grow sad and weary. He had started to face the realities of war.

"Went to the southern part of London yesterday with a couple of the fellows to find a bookstore a buddy of mine had recommended. When we got there, we found the neighborhood had been nearly decimated by German bombs. The bookstore was completely gone and a Bobby patrolling the area told us that the owner had been killed when the building collapsed. Can you believe it? A guy owns a little book shop in order to make a simple living and feed his family and in the blink of an eye, he and his shop are gone. He was doing no harm to anyone. He wasn't seen by the bombardier in a plane flying high above. With the push of a button his life, and many others are gone."

Katie stopped reading for a moment and, placing the journal face down on her lap, wiped her eyes and took a few deep breaths. She peered out the attic window and noticed that it was getting late. She really should be getting home. She would ask Ruth if it would be okay for her to borrow Ruddy's journal and take it home to study. Her bedroom would certainly be more comfortable than the White's attic and, besides, she could take her time, which would make her better able to handle the impact of reading his words.

She gently placed the box of letters, his wallet, shoes, and clothing back into the box and closed the lid.

"Now that I've done this," she said to herself. "It will be easier to come and look at his things again," and she slid the box back into its place against the wall.

Carrying the journal downstairs, she went in search of Ruth, finding her seated by herself in the library.

"There you are," Ruth said, looking up as Katie entered. "Are you alright? You were up there for quite some time."

"Yes, I'm O.K," Katie replied, wiping some dust from her skirt. "I found Ruddy's journal and couldn't resist reading some of it," and she held up the book for Ruth to see.

"Oh," was all Ruth said, holding out her hand to reach for it before stopping herself and quickly dropping it back down to her side.

"Would you like to see it?" asked Katie, putting the book down on the coffee table in front of them.

Ruth looked down at the leather journal with the gold embossed name of her older brother and shook her head.

"No, Katie," she replied, softly. "Not yet. You take it home and read it first. Search for your clues. And when you are finished, you can bring it back. Maybe I'll read it then."

Katie nodded and sat next to her friend. Placing her hand on Ruth's arm she said, "Yes, I was hoping you'd let me borrow it. I will take good care of it, of course. I must admit, it has been difficult for me to read as well, so I will need several days to summon the courage to get through it."

They sat in silence for several minutes before Ruth asked, "what else did you find in the box? Was it awful, Katie?"

Katie looked down and nodded. "Yes, it was awful," she replied, sadly. "There is his uniform dress jacket, which still has the scent of his cologne. It brought memories of him crashing back to me." Ruth took Katie's hand in hers, holding it gently as Katie continued. "There's several pieces of clothing, and a stack of letters, mostly ones I wrote to him. But the hardest thing was seeing his wallet. The Army must have removed it from his...when he was...well...they included it with the other things. I couldn't bear to bring it down so it's still up in the box. And now this journal. Reading it is hard, but it may be the only way to find out why Ruddy sent the code."

It wasn't until the next afternoon that Katie was able to pick up the journal again and continue reading. Earlier that morning, she had called Mr. Conner at the *Gazette* to tell him that she was on the trail of a big story and would be in later. Now she was seated in the sunroom hoping that the light of the beautiful day, and the nearness of Gran's rose garden, would help to keep her in good spirits as she read Ruddy's dark entries about war. However, not all his passages were dismal.

"I am the luckiest man alive!" he wrote in one of them. *"My darling Katie has agreed to the elopement! I asked her in my last letter and have been holding my breath*

until her answer came by mail today. She said yes!"

Katie thought back to the day she had received his letter asking if she would consider not waiting until the end of the war to marry him in a large elaborate ceremony, but to elope instead. He would be home on leave in a few weeks and they could get married then.

"I know that I am asking a lot from you," he had written. *"And I know that our families will be angry, and you will be the one to bear the brunt of that, but I simply cannot wait."*

She was glad that she had agreed, and that he had known and could look forward to it. She hadn't really wanted the big hoopla wedding ceremony either and, as the war dragged on, found she didn't want to wait. But, in the end, it was not meant to be. His letter had come just before his secret mission to Licata, Sicily, and then his leave was cancelled, and he received new orders that would take him to the beaches of Normandy.

Since Ruddy wrote about it in the journal, which Katie imagined would eventually be read by his family, she wondered if she should share the planned elopement with Ruthie. Would the White family feel betrayed? And how would her own grandmother feel? She supposed that she should tell her first. Oh dear.

"We completed our mission successfully," Katie read, returning to the journal. *"But the ringleader has, once again, gotten away. He is a very slippery fellow to be sure. But Baby was found intact and now resides in my breast pocket."*

Katie straightened in her chair. Here might be a clue at last! There was no doubt in her mind that he was referring to the secret mission in Licata and that "Baby" was the formula.

"Jim is not happy with me," was how Ruddy's entry began on the following day. *"He says that Baby is too dangerous to keep and that it should be destroyed immediately. I reminded him that we have orders to hand everything over to Colonel Diggins, but Jim countered that it is highly possible that we will get captured or killed and, with Baby in our possession, the enemy would have it again. It would be safer to destroy it while we have the chance."*

This jived with the story Jim had told her that evening after dinner at Rosegate.

"Kenneth and Max have sided with me and said that Baby has such good uses that it would be criminal to destroy it," Ruddy continued to write. *"Kenneth even offered to carry it himself. Jim, Matty, and Bob feel that we should destroy it. As team leader of this mission, I have decided to take possession of the valuable note myself and hand it over to the Colonel."*

There was an absence in the dates following, indicating that Ruddy had not been able to write in his journal for several days, which was understandable. His writing started again five days later.

"Something strange is happening and I don't know who to trust," he wrote. *"The day after we captured the German spy-ring, we made our way to the command post to*

hand over Baby to Colonel Diggins. He was at mess with some brass, so we were told to go stow our gear and return a few hours later. Since I had orders to hand Baby over to him directly, I kept it in my possession but when I returned, the colonel was still not there. In fact, they couldn't find him anywhere. Then, later that evening, his body was discovered about a quarter of a mile from the post. It is assumed that he was the victim of a sniper's bullet. No one knows why he would have wandered away from the post. So, I still have Baby.

We've been on the road now for five days on our way through Sicily to Caltanissetta. The fighting has been intense, and we lost Matty and Bob two days ago. Yesterday morning, it was nearly Jim's turn, but the bullet hit his helmet, and ricocheted off, embedding itself in a nearby wall. Jim stopped and dug it out, dropping it into his pocket. He told me he was going to make a charm out of it and wear it around his neck for luck.

Last night, as we slept in the woods along the roadway, I woke to see Max rifling through the pockets of my fatigue jacket which I had beside me. He told me that he was just looking for a match so that he could light his cigarette, but I don't believe him. He knows that we can't light a match at night since this could give away our location to the enemy. Fortunately, I had moved Baby to the inside of my stocking cap under my helmet. I'm not saying that Max was after it, but I plan on keeping a close eye on him."

"Max?" exclaimed Katie, softly to herself. "Could he have been after the formula for money or was he just trying to make himself more important by taking charge of it?" she wondered. She could easily imagine any one of the team doing either. Even Jim Fielding.

"Even Kenneth and Jim keep asking me about Baby," continued Ruddy. *"I suppose they're nervous about my carrying such a valuable thing throughout Europe, but there is no one I can trust but myself. So, I have come up with a plan. I'm going to mail Baby back to Sunset Hill for safe keeping. It will be hidden from everyone until I return home on leave. Perhaps Katie will agree to a honeymoon in Washington D.C. and I will have the opportunity to hand it to the Surgeon General then! I will have to write and ask her."*

Katie remembered the letter. At the time, she thought it a rather unusual request as Washington D.C. wouldn't have been on her list of honeymoon sites, but she had agreed. "I really don't care where we go," she had written him. "As long as we are together."

Another week had passed before Ruddy's next entry in his journal.

"I am tired and angry. I have just been told that all leaves are cancelled. I talked to my CO and told him that I was supposed to get married, but it was no good. He just smiled and said that he understood but that everyone in the Division was needed for a big operation coming down the pike. 'It's a tough break I know, kid,' he said to me and then told me that his wife was due to give birth to their first child in about a week and here he was. I calmed down a bit after that. I realize that I'm not the only one needing to go home. He said that he was sure my girl would understand. I hope she does. Katie, do you know how much I love and adore you?

Now, not only will I have to wait to see Katie, I will also not have a chance to hand over Baby. Just to be on the safe side, I think I'll send a message home about Baby just in case I don't make it back. Maybe a code of sorts in case my letters get intercepted. Ruth and Katie will know what to do."

Katie scanned the last several pages of the journal but Ruddy had not written any more about the formula or the numbers clue that he had sent. She closed the journal and, clasping it to her chest, made her decision.

She was going to hold a dinner party.

CHAPTER 14
THE DINNER PARTY

"A Dinner Party?" exclaimed E.M., looking up at Katie as she stood in front of his desk in the *Gazette* newsroom. "Tonight? How wonderful! Yes, of course I'll be there."

"Good," replied Katie, her hands on her hips. "Cocktails are at six."

"Formal attire, I presume?" inquired E.M., hopefully.

"Yes, I'm sorry about that," replied Katie, nodding. "Gran is rather particular about it."

"Are you kidding!" he exclaimed, rubbing his hands together. "I think it's wonderful! My tuxedo just came back from the cleaners after I wore it to Boots' party. My landlady won't know what to think when she sees me wearing it twice in one month!"

Katie smiled and was turning to walk back to her own desk when he added, "Can I assume that the evening might be filled with mystery and intrigue?"

"Gosh, I certainly hope so!" she answered, with a flip of her hand.

In another hour, she had secured the attendance of Ruth, Robert Reed, Boots, Jim Fielding, and Kenneth West.

"Miss Porter," she heard a voice call behind her. "If you're finished with your social obligations, might I see you for a moment?"

She turned to see Mr. Connor standing behind her, his hands in his pockets, a newspaper tucked under his arm. He had a mildly worried expression on his face.

"Yes, of course," she replied and, jumping to her feet, followed the editor back to his office.

He motioned her to sit down as he slid into his own chair. He took the newspaper from under his arm and plopped it down on top of his desk, flipping it open to face her.

It was a copy of the *Middleton Times.*

"Page two," he said, nodding to the paper.

Katie quickly opened to page two and there it was. A picture of her and one of E.M. There was an article that followed with the headline, "Society Gal and War Hero Save Famous Judge's Son." The long article told how Thomas White, son of Fairfield Judge James White, was pulled, unconscious, from the large fountain on the Sunset Hill Estate and revived by Katie and E.M. The *Times* included the fact that both were reporters for the *Gazette* and that E.M. was a decorated war veteran who had served as a correspondent for the *Stars and Stripes* newspaper.

"It is unclear as to why the two *Gazette* reporters were at Sunset Hill, but it was fortunate that they were. It should be noted that Miss Porter, a resident of neighboring Rosegate Estate, is a long-time friend of the White family and was once engaged to their eldest son, Rutherford White, who was killed in the Normandy Invasion. We can only assume that the visit was a social one." The article finished by saying that Thomas had suffered a broken leg and bump on the head but was recovering well at the hospital with hopes of being released soon.

Katie, who had forgotten all about Jim's warning that the story would be in the *Times*, groaned and shook her head.

"Miss Porter," sighed Mr. Connor. "As you are relatively new to the professional newspaper business perhaps you are unaware that when an interesting news story falls into a reporter's lap, the expectation is that they will cover it. And, preferably, for their own paper."

He leaned back in his chair and placed his hands behind his head.

"Mr. Connor," exclaimed Katie, embarrassed. "I really don't know what to say. E.M. and I were at Sunset Hill to visit the family when Tom fell from the top of the fountain and was knocked unconscious. I'm afraid that E.M. and I thought of nothing more than to try and save him."

"Yes, I can believe that," replied Mr. Connor. "Especially from the two of you. But what I'm trying to figure out is why it didn't occur to either of you to write about it rather than giving it to the *Times*?"

"You're right of course," said Katie, blushing. She looked down at her feet and said, "I suppose I didn't realize it *was* a news story. It would have sounded a bit like self-promotion, don't you think?"

Tom Connor lowered his arms and rocked forward, placing his palms on his desk. "Miss Porter," he began, evenly. "Sometimes a little self-promotion is a good thing, especially if it means bringing much needed readership to this newspaper. Besides, you *are* news, Miss Porter, whether you like it or not and almost everything you do gets into the local papers. So, saving a Judge's son from drowning would certainly fit the criteria of a worthy news story. But, if you don't want to write about yourself, you could have made Thomas White and the family the main focus of the article. They, themselves, are newsworthy and you had no trouble writing about their daughter's party?"

"That was different," sighed Katie. "That was a debutante party and those types of social occasions are expected to be written about. If E.M. and I hadn't covered it, the Whites would have posted an announcement in the paper."

Tom Connor looked at Katie for a few minutes and then rubbed his eyes.

"There is an angle to this that the *Times* didn't elaborate on," he said. "But it's really a good one although I'm sure E.M. would have been reluctant to use it." He paused for a moment to think, and then continued, "yes, I'm positive that he won't want us to use it. However, you could have written that part about him and he could have written the stuff about you."

"And what angle is that, Mr. Connor?" Katie asked, gazing over at him with curiosity.

"This was not E.M.'s first drowning rescue," he replied, once again leaning back in his chair and returning his hands to the back of his head. "When E.M. Butler was serving as a correspondent during the war, he was a young officer with the *Stars and Stripes* and stationed in London. During one of the many bombing raids on the city, the building where E.M. happened to be working was hit and collapsed trapping him and several people, all of whom were injured, inside."

Katie leaned forward in her chair and gasped.

"They could have stayed put until the raid was over, of course," continued Mr. Connor. "Had the main water pipe not been crushed and water started flooding the entire basement where the group was located. Three fellow servicemen, two women, one a pregnant secretary and the other an aide worker with two refugee children in tow, would have surely drowned had E.M. not saved every single last one of them by carrying them out of the building one at a time to safety."

"I would have been scared out of my wits!" exclaimed Katie, bringing her hands to her face.

"He was, Miss Porter," replied the editor. "Terrified! But that didn't deter him from doing what needed to be done. He was awarded the Bronze Star for his heroism and, after the war, could have gotten a job with any paper he wanted but he came here. I don't understand why and all he will tell me is that he likes the countryside. He also doesn't talk about what happened, but I know it affected him greatly and I'm willing to bet he thinks about it often."

"Well then, Mr. Connor," said Katie, getting up from her chair and looking at her editor with determination. "I'm glad that E.M. and I didn't write the story. I would have had no problem with E.M. writing about me but, honestly, I was not the most important part of the story. I just happened to be standing near Tom when he hit the bottom of the basin and I was able to reach over and hold his head above the water. It was E.M. who lifted him out of the fountain and began the resuscitation, giving me instructions on how to cradle Tom's head throughout the entire process. Afterwards, E.M. was literally shaking and, when I asked him about it, all he told me was that it was post-war nerves."

"But Miss Porter," began Mr. Connor, somewhat gruffly. "What about the *Middleton Times*! They…"

"Let them wallow in the mud," interrupted Katie. "Leave us to honor the wishes of a real war hero and Bronze Star recipient." She started toward the door and then stopped and turned. "Besides, Mr. Connor," she said smiling. "I'm working on a story that's going to curl your hair!" and she left the office, closing the door gently behind her.

Mr. Connor stared after her and, running a hand over his closely cropped hair, hoped she was right.

* * *

"I hope you don't mind, Katie dear," began her grandmother, as she clipped on an earring, and addressed Katie's reflection in her dressing table mirror. "But I invited my old friend, Mr. Henderson, to your dinner party tonight."

"Excellent idea, Gran!" replied Katie, giving her a warm smile. "I should have thought of inviting him myself."

Mr. Adolpho Henderson was a friendly gentleman of about seventy years old and a close friend of Mrs. Porter. He lived in Fairfield but, as a world traveler, was often away. When he was home, Katie and her grandmother would often ask him to dine with them, enjoying his lively sense of humor and his tales of adventure in far off places.

"He's coming a little early so that I may show him my new Mister Lincoln's," added Mrs. Porter, standing and gazing at her own reflection as she smoothed down her dress. "He'll be here at five-thirty so I shall tell Andrews to decant the whiskey."

"And I must hurry and finish getting ready," replied Katie, rushing to her own room. Once there, she threw open her closet and carefully reviewed her wardrobe. She wanted to wear just the right dress for the occasion. She settled on a royal blue grown with a scoop neckline and tapered waist. The color always brought out the color of her eyes and the neckline would accommodate the ornate necklace that Gran had given her for her birthday.

However, when she went to remove the locket that the White family had given her, she found that she simply couldn't do it. She hadn't taking it off since Tom had helped her put it on the day of Boots' debutante party.

"Tonight is the perfect night to keep it on," she decided. "I'll need Ruddy's help, now more than ever." Slipping on a pair of silver slippers, she took a final look at herself in the mirror.

"Perfect," she smiled. "Now I'm ready."

When she came downstairs, she found that Mr. Henderson had already arrived and was admiring her grandmother's roses out in the garden.

"These are wonderful, Agatha," he was saying, while bending to sniff a bloom. "What on earth do you do to make them so healthy?"

"Now, Adolpho," replied Mrs. Porter, shaking a finger at him with mock sternness. "You know I can't disclose those secrets. I can't afford any competition at this year's Rose Show."

"I believe that you will not face any competition with roses as fine as these," he smiled charmingly back at her.

Mrs. Porter did not reply and looked away, but Katie caught enough of a glimpse to see that her grandmother was blushing slightly.

"Mr. Henderson," she said, by way of announcing her presence. "Are you flirting with my grandmother?" She stepped into the garden, a smile on her face, and her hand extended.

"Katie!" exclaimed Mr. Henderson, his gaze taking her in. "Is that you? My darling child, you're gorgeous!"

Now it was Katie's turn to blush, but she continued forward to shake his hand. "You are quite the charmer, Mr. Henderson."

"Which is why you and your grandmother invite me here so often," he teased, taking both their arms in his.

They strolled back inside, through the sunroom, and into the long hallway of the Rosegate mansion. As they neared the library, they heard the front doorbell ring and the steady steps of Andrews as he approached to answer.

"Mr. Butler," he announced, turning and facing Mrs. Porter and Katie.

E.M. stepped around him and paused to remove his hat, coat, and gloves, handing them to the butler who took them and quietly disappeared.

"E.M.!" greeted Katie, walking over to her friend. "You're just in time! And, my, don't you look dashing!"

He had rushed to get a haircut and shave after receiving her invitation that afternoon and was dressed in his fine fitting tuxedo, perfectly shined shoes, and a white carnation in his lapel.

He took Katie's hand and rocked back to take a look at her. "And you look absolutely ravishing! I love that color on you. Dior?"

"Yes," replied Katie, chuckling. "I must say you certainly know your designers," she added, patting his hand as they approached Mrs. Porter and Mr. Henderson.

"Mrs. Porter," said E.M., giving Katie's grandmother a little bow. "It's wonderful to see you again."

"And you," replied Mrs. Porter. "We're so glad you could make it. May I present my old friend, Mr. Adolpho Henderson. Adolpho, this is Katie's friend, Mr. E.M. Butler."

"A pleasure, sir," said E.M. shaking Mr. Henderson's outstretched hand.

"The pleasure is all mine," returned Adolpho. "I am always interested in meeting Katie's friends. As her surrogate grandfather, it is my duty to make sure they are worthy of her friendship," he added, winking at Katie.

Katie sighed and her grandmother patted Mr. Henderson's arm and whispered, "hush, Adolpho!" but E.M. just smiled and replied, "Well, I'm not sure there is anyone completely worthy of Katie's friendship except, perhaps, Miss. Ruth White but I will endeavor to earn it."

"Ah! Excellent answer, young man," Mr. Henderson replied. "You have already earned several points in your favor."

Before Katie could make a response, Andrews announced from the front door, "Dr. Reed, Miss Ruth White, and Miss Margaret White."

As the group relinquished their coats and hats to Andrews, Katie stepped forward to greet them. As introductions were being made, Katie asked Robert Reed about Tom's condition.

"He's doing very well," replied the doctor. "Although the leg is going to take some time to heal." Reaching out to take Ruth's hand, he added, "we do need to get him out of the hospital as soon as possible, though, because he's been flirting with all of the nurses and they are finding it hard to tend to other patients."

"Oh dear," chuckled Katie. "So even a brush with death hasn't taught him anything."

"Apparently not," agreed Ruth, as the group turned and entered the library.

There were enjoying cocktails and an entertaining story by Adolpho, when Andrews stepped into the room and announced the arrival of Jim Fielding and Kenneth West.

"Our apologies, Mrs. Porter," Jim said, walking over to Katie's grandmother, and then nodding to Katie, "Miss Porter. I had a bit of car trouble this afternoon and it took several hours for the mechanic to fix it. I'm afraid it held us up."

"Apology not necessary, Mr. Fielding," replied Katie. "You are still in time for cocktails. Please allow me to introduce you and Mr. West to Dr. Reed and Mr. Henderson."

The two men were introduced first to Ruth's fiancé who warmly shook their hands but when it came to Mr. Henderson, there was a strange exchange between him and Kenneth West. It was as if the two men had met before but weren't quite sure.

"Mr. Heinrick, did you say?" asked Kenneth West, looking directly into

Adolpho's eyes as he gripped his hand.

"No, Henderson," repeated Adolpho, turning pale.

"Sorry, my mistake," replied Kenneth, turning to take a cocktail offered him from a tray held by Andrews.

The awkward exchange did not escape Katie's notice. "Things should start to get very interesting," she said to herself as dinner was announced.

The conversation at dinner was as lively as the food was good.

"Where on earth did your cook get such a wonderful cut of pork?" Ruth asked Katie, cutting easily into the chop. "Mildred is still finding it difficult so soon after the war."

"I think it's more a matter of Gertie being able to turn anything into something edible," replied Katie, putting down her wine glass. "During the war, she was a wizard with shoe leather."

"Really?" said a horrified Boots. "Shoe leather?"

"Katie is just teasing, Margaret," replied Mrs. Porter, giving Katie a stern look. "We never ate shoe leather." Then, after pausing to take a sip from her glass, she added, "although Gertie's shoelaces were simply delicious."

Everyone at the table burst into laughter, all except Boots who looked around in confusion.

"I remember when I was in Switzerland during the war," said E.M. "Everyone raved about this little café in Lucerne that was supposed to have this wonderful locally made noodle dish. Being a devout lover of food, I couldn't wait to try it. So, one day, I hitched a ride with a Swiss farmer who was on his way to market. It was a terribly hot day and the farmer's truck was uncomfortable, bouncing us over the rough road. When I finally got to the café, I sat down and ordered the noodle dish, barely able to contain myself in anticipation. It seemed as though I waited forever, but when the dish came is looked and smelled wonderful. There in front of me was a bowl of wheat noodles, covered in white cream sauce, with three large Asparagus laying across the top."

The group around the table leaned forward listening intently to E.M.'s description.

"Well you can imagine how I felt," he continued. "I'd been eating Army K-rations for weeks. I thought I'd died and gone to heaven. So, with my mouth watering, I picked up my fork and dove into the noodles bringing them up and into my mouth. And you know what?" he asked, looking around the room. "They tasted exactly like someone's shoelaces!"

Chuckles and groans were heard around the table and Boots shook her head at him.

"What a shame," said Ruth, picking up her fork again. "To look forward to a delicious meal and then not be able to eat it."

"Who said anything about not eating it?" chuckled E.M. "Those shoelace noodles were the best thing I had eaten in a long time. I licked the plate clean!"

There was another round of laughter, and then Kenneth West looked over at Mr. Henderson and said, "Jim, Mr. Butler, and I all served in Europe during the war. What did you do, sir?"

Adolpho glanced around the table and replied softly, "I was with the International Red Cross in Paris, during that city's occupation by the Germans. I speak both French and German." When he didn't add anything further an awkward silence filled the room causing Katie to quickly push back her chair and stand.

"Let's all go into the game room for some coffee and entertainment. Ruthie has promised to play the piano for us."

The group retired to the comfortable chairs of the Porter's game room. It was Katie's favorite room in the house; cheery with large windows, a tall ceiling, a stately fireplace, which was currently without a fire due to the spring weather outside, and a beautiful Steinway grand piano that stood in the corner.

Although Katie played, Ruth was the real musician, and she graciously sat down behind the keyboard and entertained them with several numbers, all of which were met with enthusiastic applause.

Halfway through the recital, Katie gave Ruth a subtle nod. It was time to spring her trap. She stood and addressed her assembled guests.

"Ladies and gentlemen," she began, "I have just recently discovered that one of our group is a wonderful singer. It would be a shame not to take advantage of this musical evening and hear him."

There was a murmur of voices as everyone looked around. Ruth waited at the piano, her hands resting in her lap.

"Mr. Fielding, would you please come up and honor us with a song?" said Katie, waving her hand in the direction of the piano, a gleam in her eye.

"No, really," began Jim, putting up his hands in protest. "I haven't sung…."

But the clapping of the group made it impossible for him to refuse and, shooting Katie a glance, his eyebrows raised, he stepped over and stood next to the piano.

"Is there a particular song that Miss Porter wishes me to sing?" he asked, as Katie once again took her seat.

"Well, let me see," she pretended to ponder for a moment. "How about *I'll be seeing you.* That's always been one of my favorites."

"Mine too," smiled Jim, and turning to Ruth, said, "key of G, please, Miss White."

Other than to find out if this Jim Fielding was really the Jim Fielding that Ruddy called his friend, Katie was not sure what she expected. She certainly didn't count on the absolute beauty of Jim's tenor voice which took her breath away and brought tears to her eyes. Ruddy had not been exaggerating. This guy's singing could simply knock you off your chair and Katie was enthralled.

When Jim finished the number and started toward his chair, the group jumped to their feet and begged him to sing a few more songs. He looked first at Katie, who could only nod, and then apologetically at Ruth, but she was clapping enthusiastically along with the rest.

Shrugging his shoulders, he once again stood by the piano. This time he selected the song and leaned in to whisper it to Ruthie, who nodded.

These Foolish Things was another wartime favorite and his audience leaned forward, thoroughly enjoying his rendition. When he looked directly at Katie and sang the words, "those stumbling words that told you what my heart meant," she thought that she might faint.

However, a gasp from Mr. Henderson, and the sound of his chair crashing to the floor as he fell out of it, stopped that from happening. Everyone stood in shocked silence for a moment before Robert Reed came running toward the prone man, with Jim close on his heels.

Adolpho Henderson was clawing at his neck, his face turning a deep red as he gasped for air. While Robert ran out to his car to get his medical bag, Jim untied Mr. Henderson's bow tie and unbuttoned the top button of his dress shirt. Suddenly Adolpho raised a hand and pulled him down so that he could whisper in Jim's ear. Then he lost consciousness completely.

Andrews must have been lingering just outside the door because he had known to call for an ambulance and one was at the door in record time. Mr. Henderson was on a stretcher and on his way to the hospital before everyone could fully absorb what had just happened.

"A heart attack, I suspect," said Dr. Reed, putting on his hat and coat. "I'm sorry darling but I'll have to go to the hospital with him," he added, bending down to give Ruth a quick kiss.

"I'll have to go too," exclaimed Mrs. Porter. "He doesn't have any family in town. Katie will you drive me, please?"

"Yes, certainly," Katie replied, as everyone followed her into the hallway to gather their things.

She had pulled the roadster close to the mansion and was waiting for her grandmother when Jim Fielding suddenly appeared at her window. He had left Kenneth waiting in the car, parked a few feet away.

"Miss Porter," he said gravely. "I think you should know what Mr. Henderson whispered in my ear."

"Yes?" she replied, glancing at the front door as her grandmother, assisted by Andrews, made her way outside.

"He said a name," replied Jim Fielding in a whisper. "*Der Rabe.*"

CHAPTER 15
CONIUM MACULATUM

"Before we go any further," exclaimed Katie forcefully. "I'm going to need you to unbutton your shirt."

They were sitting on a bench the following morning, beside the large pond in the center of Fairfield's central park. The shade from a nearby tree protected them from the sun, adding to the refreshing coolness of a breeze that swept through Katie's hair.

"I beg your pardon," replied Jim, startled. "You want me to do what?"

"I need to see what you're wearing around your neck," she demanded.

"Oh, I see," he said, smiling, and loosening his tie, he undid the top two buttons of his shirt, and reaching inside, pulled out the chain that was draped around him. Hanging from it was a crumpled bullet.

He held it up for her to see but did not remove the chain from around his neck.

"Satisfied?" he asked, tucking the bullet and chain back inside his shirt and buttoning it back up again.

"Yes," said Katie, softly, and she looked down at the journal in her lap. "I'm sorry Mr. Fielding. I just needed to make sure."

"I understand," he replied, just as softly. "Now there is something I need from you."

She looked up at him, an expression of alarm spreading across her face.

"No, no, Miss Porter," he smiled and held up his hand. "You needn't worry. I don't need to see what you're wearing around your neck. I'm fairly certain I can guess what's in the locket."

"Then what?" Katie replied, somewhat relieved.

"Would you please lean forward so that I might take a peek behind your right ear?" he requested.

She was puzzled but she did as he asked and leaned toward him. He gently pushed her hair away from her right ear and looked.

"Just as Ruddy told me," he said, letting her go. "You have a tiny scar behind your ear where he accidently hit you with a rock when you were eight years old."

"Oh, I'd forgotten!" she chuckled, unconsciously reaching up to trace the scar with her fingers. "He says it was an accident, but he always had pretty good aim, so we all believed he did it to get my attention. Instead, he got a whipping from Poppy and I got five stitches."

They sat in reflective silence for several minutes before Jim finally asked, "So, now that we've confirmed each other's identities, am I to assume that you found Ruddy's journal and that's what's resting in your lap?"

"Yes," she replied, lifting the book and handing it to him. "He wrote of the first time he met you and how beautifully you could sing. He was right," she added, looking into his eyes.

"So, last night you set me up?" he asked with a grin, opening the journal and flipping through the first few pages.

"I'm afraid so," Katie admitted. "After reading some of Ruddy's entries, I had to make sure you were you. Then it occurred to me that you could really be a German spy who happened to have a fantastic voice. So that's why I asked to see the bullet. Ruddy wrote about that too."

Jim nodded and looked over at her. "Fair enough," he replied. "After all, I had seen a picture of you, but you would have had no idea what I looked like."

"Yes, that's right," she answered. "And if you turn to the last several pages, you will see that Ruddy became very suspicious of the members of the team. It looks like he didn't trust anyone. Anyone except you, perhaps."

Jim turned to a page that Katie pointed out to him and read the entry. Frowning, he turned to the next page and continued to read.

"This explains why he sent the formula home to Sunset Hill," he said thoughtfully, finally closing the journal and handing it back to Katie. "I am truly relieved to see that he had no intention of selling it for profit."

"Yes, I am relieved as well," replied Katie, nodding her head. "Although I never really believed that he would have done such a thing. He also explains why he sent his sister and me the numbers code. It was added insurance in case he didn't make it back."

"Unfortunately, he didn't count on two things," said Jim, grimly. "That we would have so much difficulty in deciphering the darn "In The Ring" code and, secondly, that someone else, perhaps *Der Rabe* himself, would come to Sunset Hill in search of the formula."

"True," agreed Katie, bringing up her hand to grasp the locket around her neck. "Mr. Henderson whispered "*Der Rabe*" in your ear before he lost consciousness. I wonder if he was trying to tell us that the spy leader is in Fairfield? I wonder how he'd know?"

"Your guess is as good as mine," shrugged Jim. "But I'd be very grateful to know one way or the other."

"We need to solve this puzzle quickly and find the formula ourselves," said Katie, with renewed determination. "Or expose *Der Rabe* and have him arrested before he finds it and disappears again."

"So, where do we start?" asked Jim, standing and turning to look at her.

"How about a little horseback riding? Say one o'clock at my place?" replied Katie, with a twinkle in her eye.

"As long as my horse keeps its shoes," answered Jim Fielding, smiling down at her. "I'd rather not walk."

On her way back to the *Gazette*, Katie stopped at the hospital to check on Mr. Henderson. He was sleeping but she was able to pull Robert aside and get an update on the poor man's condition.

"*Conium maculatum*," said the doctor, signing the bottom of a patient's record.

"In English, please Robert," sighed Katie. "What exactly is "crownad muscular", or whatever it was you just said?"

Robert Reed chuckled and, taking Katie by the elbow, guided her towards the nurse's station.

"*Conium maculatum*, or as it is referred to in English, poison hemlock," he told her, handing the folder to the nurse behind the desk. He slid his hands into his lab coat and looked intently at Katie. "At first, I just assumed that Mr. Henderson was having a heart attack or some sort of respiratory episode. But, just to make sure, I ran some tests and, much to my surprise, there were traces of the poison in his bloodstream."

"How strange!" exclaimed Katie, rather shocked. "How would someone get something like that in their bloodstream?"

"It's ingested," replied Robert. "Most likely through tea or some other liquid."

"We had coffee right after dinner, if you remember," Katie said thoughtfully. "In the game room while listening to Ruthie play."

"Yes, that's right," said Robert, nodding. "And enjoying the delightful voice of Mr. Fielding," he added, giving Katie a sly smile.

"Yes," she replied, quickly. "So, a pill could have been slipped into Mr. Henderson's coffee by someone while his attention was elsewhere."

"It's possible, of course," replied Robert. "But it won't be in pill form. Poison hemlock is a plant with leaves, you see. It would have had to be ground up into very fine flakes if Mr. Henderson was to drink it without noticing."

"Unless he knew it was there," said Katie, bringing a hand to her chin. "And drank it anyway."

"Suicide?" asked the doctor.

"It's a possibility," replied Katie. "Mr. Henderson has no family close by. In fact, I'm not sure he has any family at all. He loves to travel but, perhaps, that was becoming difficult for him as he got older. He is very close to my grandmother. Would it be unreasonable to want to die surrounded by friends while listening to the golden tones of Mr. Fielding?"

"But it seems a very bad and relatively uncertain way to go, Katie," countered Robert, shaking his head doubtfully. "Besides, poison hemlock doesn't grow here in the United States. It'd be nearly impossible to get it."

"Where does it grow?" she asked.

"Europe and parts of North Africa," replied Robert, and then realization hit him. "Oh, I see! Mr. Henderson was a world traveler!"

"Yes, indeed," echoed Katie, nodding. "But before we jump to conclusions, Mr. Fielding and Mr. West were both in Europe during the war."

"As was your friend, Mr. Butler," added the doctor, turning to go. "Thankfully, no matter how it got into his coffee, he'll fully recover. I want to keep him under observation for a little while longer but then he'll be released."

"Gran will be so pleased!" replied Katie, smiling. "I'm sure she'll insist on him staying with us at Rosegate for several days until we can be sure he's alright. That way, we can keep an eye on him!"

"Perfect!" said Robert Reed, from halfway down the hall. "And don't forget to stop in and scold my future brother-in-law before you leave," he added as he disappeared around the corner.

The weather was as beautiful in the afternoon as it had been that morning, and Katie and Jim were having a pleasant ride across the fields on horseback. They had started out at Rosegate, riding horses from the Porter's stables, and were now on their way to Sunset Hill which, if one used the back pastures and field paths, was only seven miles away.

"Do you often go riding?" asked Jim, moving his horse alongside Katie's as they left a narrow path and entered a large field.

"As often as I can," she responded. "I love riding, especially in this back country. I find it relaxing."

"I can see why you would," he replied, glancing around him. "It's beautiful here. I never knew Fairfield had such lovely and extensive acreage. The curse of living in town, I suppose."

"I won't blame it strictly on that, Mr. Fielding," explained Katie. "About eighty percent of the undeveloped land around here is privately owned. Townspeople wouldn't have access to it even if they knew it existed."

Jim let out a whistle. "I see," he said. "And who owns this beautiful field?" he asked, looking around again, with renewed interest.

"My grandmother, Mr. Fielding," Katie replied, shooting him a glance to see if he was teasing her. The look on his face told her he wasn't. "We're still on the Rosegate Estate."

"Good Lord, Miss Porter!" he exclaimed. "How rich are you, exactly?"

"That's a rather personal question, Mr. Fielding!" replied Katie sternly, but there was a gleam in her eye. "But, if you must know, my grandmother is very, my parents, quite a bit, and me, somewhat."

"I am sorry," said Jim, quite contrite. "You are correct, it is none of my business and that was a very rude question. I'm afraid my senses left me for a minute. But, now that I know how well off you are, I'll try to be nicer to you in the future."

"That's rather disappointing, Mr. Fielding," said Katie, pretending to frown. "I rather like being your archrival."

"Ah, but you are," replied Jim, chuckling. "That doesn't mean we can't be nice about it."

They approached another narrow path and Jim slowed his horse and fell behind Katie. This made conversation difficult, so they rode in silence for several minutes. When they came out the other side and into a pasture, Katie slowed so that Jim could pull alongside. "Tell me, Mr. Fielding, does your fiancée ride?" she asked him.

"My fiancée?" he repeated, startled.

"Yes, your fiancée," Katie asked again. "Jane Manning mentioned that her brooch matched one owned by your fiancée. So, since you seem to be an avid horseman, I was wondering if she, too, liked to ride?"

"Oh, I see," he replied, grinning. "I don't have a fiancée, Miss Porter, as you've probably already guessed since I tend to show up at social occasions stag. I use an imaginary fiancée when I perceive that a young woman might be taking an extra interest in my marital status."

"I did wonder about that," smiled Katie, nodding. "Now we're even as far as rude personal questions go."

"Truce?" asked Jim, extending his hand out to her.

"Yes, truce," she responded, extending hers to shake his.

They dismounted at the edge of a stream to permit their horses to take a drink. Katie reached into her saddlebag and brought out a thermos of cold lemonade, two cups, and two muffins.

"Gertie never lets me leave home without nourishment," she chuckled, and motioned Jim over to a fallen log. "She packed enough for both of us."

"I think I'm in love with Gertie," said Jim, flopping down and unwrapping the muffin that Katie had handed him. "This is wonderful."

"I'll be sure to tell her," she replied. "Now is a good time to tell you what I've learned so far about our case," she added, handing him a cup of lemonade. "I stopped by the hospital to check on Mr. Henderson and Robert told me that it wasn't a heart attack after all. The poor man had drunk poison hemlock."

"Hemlock?" asked Jim, puzzled. "I didn't think you could find hemlock anymore."

"Not here in the US," replied Katie. "You never could. But you can in Europe, where it grows as a native plant."

"Europe?" repeated Jim, scratching his chin. "Do we have any idea when he drank it and why? And, most importantly, who put it in his drink?"

"He drank it last evening while listening to you sing," replied Katie. "In our game room. It was dropped into his coffee. We don't know why or by whom, but the suspect list is rather long."

"Oh, yes? Well let's see," said Jim, counting on his fingers. "It could be your butler Andrews, Dr. Reed, Mr. Butler, Kenneth West, me, you, and perhaps, your grandmother. I think we can rule out Boots because I just don't believe her capable of such a thing, and her sister, Ruth, since she was at the piano for most of the evening's entertainment."

"Please be serious, Mr. Fielding," sighed Katie, swatting away a fly.

"I am, Miss Porter. Let's be unemotionally analytical," he replied, patting her arm. "Let's examine the facts. Andrews had opportunity since he was the one to serve us. It would have been very easy."

"Except for two things," interrupted Katie. "One, he's been with us for thirty years and has yet to poison anybody, even with plenty of opportunity. Secondly, where on earth would he get poison hemlock?"

"Yes, well," smiled Jim. "I think it's safe to cross him off our list. I never really suspected him anyway. Now let's see, there's Dr. Reed. Doctors have ways of getting hold of all kinds of things and, being a medical man, would know how to best administer the hemlock."

"I refuse to believe that Ruth would agree to marry a murderer," replied Katie.

"My dear Miss Porter," said Jim. "Murderers are often husbands."

"What makes you say that, Mr. Fielding?" asked Katie, taking a bite of muffin.

"Because husbands are often married to wives," answered Jim, his eyes twinkling.

Katie glared at him for a moment and then burst out laughing.

"Now I understand why you're still single," she said, brushing a stray strand of hair from her face and tucking it behind her ear. "Seriously though, I believe our only two suspects are Mr. West and Mr. Henderson himself, although I simply can't believe my grandmother's old friend is a German spy."

"We can't be sure of anything these days," replied Jim, shrugging his shoulders. "I do recall some tension between the two at dinner," he added after a moment.

"Yes, I noticed that as well," agreed Katie. "But I know of no connection between the two of them, do you?"

"No," answered Jim, shaking his head. "None that I am aware of. However, this might explain why Mr. Henderson's last conscious words to me were *"Der Rabe."* He may have been trying to tell us that Kenneth is the spy, or he is admitting his own guilt because he thought he was going to die."

"Going to his grave with a clear conscious," replied Katie, nodding thoughtfully, then glancing at her wristwatch. "Well, I think we should get going."

They returned the thermos, cups, and muffin wrappings back to Katie's saddlebag and mounted their horses. Riding side by side, Katie continued, "I think we can cross off you, E.M., and myself," she told him. "And don't even think of accusing my grandmother!"

Jim chuckled, "O.K. I concede your grandmother, although she could be growing Poison Hemlock between her roses bushes and, I imagine, could kill someone who posed enough of a threat. Especially if that threat was directed at you."

Katie shot him a glance. "Yes, I'd remember that if I were you, Mr. Fielding," she added with a smile.

Jim smiled back at her. "O.K., Mrs. Porter is off the list, but I refuse to cross off Mr. Butler."

Before Katie could reply, they spotted a man walking slowly up ahead. He wore a tweed suit and hat and was using a walking stick.

"We've just crossed over into Mr. Wellington's property," Katie whispered. "He won't mind but I do like to ask his permission, anyway."

As they rode up to the elderly gentleman, Katie waved and yelled, "Hello, Mr. Wellington! Lovely day, isn't it?"

"Why hello there, Miss Katie!" replied Mr. Wellington. "Yes, indeed, a beautiful day," and he removed his hat and rested it against his chest.

"This is my friend, Mr. Fielding," she said, introducing Jim. "We're on our way over to Sunset Hill. May we cross your pasture?"

"Why certainly, Miss," answered Mr. Wellington, with a nod of his head. "You know you're always welcome. Thanks for asking, though. Not everyone does. These young people these days just march across as if they own the place!"

"Yes, how unfortunate," said Katie, already nudging her horse forward.

"Why just an hour ago a man came through with a shovel resting on his shoulder and walking rapidly," continued Mr. Wellington. "He was a bit far from me, so I yelled to him and asked where he thought he was going. He yelled back, 'to Sunset Hill to dig for treasure'. Imagine that, Miss Katie! It's bad enough that they march through someone else's property but now they think they can dig it up!"

Jim and Katie froze in their tracks.

"What did this man look like?" asked Jim, concerned. "Have you ever seen him before?"

"I couldn't say," replied Mr. Wellington, placing his hat back on his head. "He was further than my eyes can see, and the way he was carrying that shovel, well, I decided not to tangle with him."

Jim and Katie exchanged looks as Mr. Wellington slowly turned to leave.

"Oh yes, one more thing," he added, turning back to look at them. "Rather strange. I heard him singing as he walked down the trail away from me."

"Why is that strange, Mr. Wellington?" asked Katie. "Lots of people sing while walking through a lovely field like yours on a beautiful day."

"Not in German, Miss Katie," replied the old gentleman. "Any other language, maybe, but most people don't speak German this soon after the war if they know what's good for them."

CHAPTER 16
THE RACE IS ON!

They urged their horses forward, trotting through the narrow paths, and then into a full gallop whenever they reached an open field. There was a renewed sense of urgency. The German spy, *Der Rabe*, was among them.

When they arrived at the edge of the Sunset Hill Estate, Jim motioned for them to stop.

"We've got to proceed with great care," he cautioned. "And stay together. This man is extremely dangerous."

"Agreed," replied Katie, breathlessly. "I sure don't want to encounter him alone. What should we do first?"

"Would it be unusual for the White family to see you riding around their estate on horseback without an invitation or the presence of a family member?" asked Jim, glancing at the house which stood a good distance away.

"No, I have an open invitation and have often ridden here through the years. Besides, they consider me a member of their family," she replied. "However, I always stop in to say hello before I leave even if it's very briefly."

"Excellent," Jim replied, with a nod of his head. "That gives us time to look around before we need to engage with the family."

"Look there!" Katie said suddenly, pointing to the ground. "I think those might be his tracks."

Along the edge of the trail were tracks obviously made by a man. They seemed to turn right and then disappear along the tree line, only to reappear on areas of dirt or ruffled grass. Jim and Katie slowly rode along, following the footprints as best they could. Occasionally they would stop to listen for the sounds of someone digging but heard nothing but the wind in the trees and, in the distance, Mad Uncle Henry flying back and forth from his birdhouse perch and the main house. Katie easily spotted the beautiful colors of his expanded wings as he flew.

"Look over there," whispered Jim, pointing to a clearing in the woods. He and Katie dismounted and, securing the reins of their horses to a nearby tree limb, walked quietly into the clearing to investigate. They found three holes that had been dug recently.

"I wonder why he chose this spot," murmured Jim, scratching his head and glancing around.

"Perhaps because this clearing creates a nearly perfect ring of trees," replied Katie, slowly waving her hand around the circle. "Which means that our spy knows about Ruddy's clue."

"And that fact continues to incriminate Kenneth and E.M. Butler," reminded Jim, thoughtfully. "Although it looks like Mr. Henderson is now out of contention."

"I asked E.M. if he was *Der Rabe* and he denied it," explained Katie, in defense of her friend. "Though, if he really was the spy leader, I suppose he'd have no scruples in lying about his identity. But still, I just can't believe it!"

"I know how you feel, Miss Porter," replied Jim. "It's hard for me to swallow the fact that Kenneth might be the spy because he was a member of our team that captured the spy ring in Licata."

"But the leader wasn't there, if I recall," countered Katie, bending down to examine the holes. "He could have been a traitor among you even then." She stood and, brushing her hands on her Jodhpurs, declared, "we must solve this puzzle soon!"

They explored the property on horseback for nearly two hours, stopping anywhere that was "ring-like" and where a formula could be hidden or examining anything that looked like a recently dug hole for clues on *Der Rabe.* But, in the end, they realized that Sunset Hill was far too large an estate for them to make much progress.

"This is like looking for a needle in a haystack," exclaimed Katie in frustration. "Surely there's a better way to do this!"

"Is there a high point on the property that might serve as a vantage point?" asked Jim, bringing his horse alongside hers. "A place where we could see the entire property and be able to narrow our search. We might even spot *Der Rabe.*"

"No, there's no such vantage point on the grounds" replied Katie, suddenly turning her horse. "But there is on the roof of the Sunset Hill mansion!" she cried over her shoulder as she galloped away.

Jim gave his horse a gentle kick and was soon galloping close behind her as the two raced toward the main house. As they approached, Katie slowed her horse to a trot and veered off to the left toward the stables with Jim following. Once there, they dismounted and handed the reins to one of the stable hands.

"Hello, Phillip," said Katie, greeting the young man who came out to take charge of the horses. "Would you please see that our horses get some water and shade? Mr. Fielding and I may be a while."

"Yes, Miss," replied Phillip, leading both horses away.

Jim and Katie proceeded to the mansion and entered through the large patio door. Just inside sat Tom White in a wheelchair, looking morose, his leg in a cast from his ankle to his hip.

"Why, hello Tom," said Katie, bending down to give him a quick peck on the forehead. "It's good to see you home. How are you feeling?"

"Terrible!" Tom replied. "I have no one to keep me company except Mad Uncle Henry, I'm missing my card game with the fellas, and this cast on my leg is driving me crazy," he added, slapping the side of it.

"I must say, old man," chuckled Jim, looking down at him. "It is a very impressive cast. Must weigh a ton."

Tom glowered at him. "Yes, it does!" he exclaimed. "I swear Robert put it on me just so that I couldn't do anything or go anywhere."

"If that were the case, you should feel lucky it's not a ball and chain," teased Katie, passing him and walking in the direction of the hallway.

"Might as well be," Tom replied, sullenly.

"We're going up to the roof," shouted Katie over her shoulder. "I want to show Mr. Fielding the view."

"Oh, is that what we're calling it these days?" Tom joked. "I'll have to remember that next time I bring a young lady…"

"Don't be impertinent, Tom White," Jim quickly said before the young man could finish his sentence. "Or you'll be wearing a cast on the other leg." He followed Katie out of the room and toward the staircase that led up to the roof.

"We used to often come up to the roof as kids," explained Katie, glancing over her shoulder as she and Jim climbed the long staircase. "To play or sit and read. When we got older, it was a great place to talk privately or…well…let's just say that Tom isn't too far off," she added with a grin. Jim noticed a slight blush creeping across her face just before she turned and pushed open the door to the attic.

"We have to walk through the attic to reach the outside door," she explained to Jim's puzzled expression. "Watch your step and the dust."

They walked to the opposite end of the room where Katie opened the door that led to the mansion's roof.

"Here we are! Oh, sorry Ruth," she exclaimed. "I didn't expect to see you up here!"

Ruth White was standing next to Robert Reed, their arms around each other, gazing out over the lawn.

"I could say the same of you," replied Ruth, her eyebrows rising when she saw Jim stepping through the door behind Katie.

"Yes, well," Katie stammered. "Mr. Fielding and I need to survey the estate from as high up as possible."

"Well you can't get much higher than here," smiled Robert. "Hello Mr. Fielding."

Jim nodded at both Ruth and Robert. "We're trying to see if there is anything that resembles a ring or is ring-shaped. A clearing in the woods, a pond, your circular driveway."

"Oh, I see," replied Ruth. "Ruddy's code. That makes sense," and she turned to gaze out onto the expansive acreage of Sunset Hill.

"Ruddy's code?" asked Robert, looking over at his fiancée.

"It's rather a long story, Robert," replied Ruthie, looking affectionately up into his eyes. "Let's go down for some iced tea and I'll tell you all about it."

"Wow!" exclaimed Jim Fielding, after Ruth and Robert had left. "This is great, Miss Porter! We can see for miles up here."

"Yes," replied Katie, shading her eyes from the sun with her hand. "If you stand over there and take the south side, I'll take the north."

They separated, each positioning themselves on opposite sides of the roof. The view was not new to Katie, of course, but she now looked at it with a new perspective, searching for areas that might fit Ruddy's description in the code.

Jim, however, was looking at the view for the first time and was enthralled by the beauty of the rolling green hills and deep woods. There appeared to be no end to the Sunset Hill Estate and that fact, in and of itself, seemed to make their current task nearly impossible.

Katie was beginning to feel the same way. Nothing ring-shaped appeared as she looked across the acreage. Finally, shrugging, she stepped back from her vantage point to join Jim on the south side of the roof.

"Do you see anything of interest?" she asked him, coming up to stand beside him.

"Yes, thousands of things that are of interest," he replied, scanning the horizon. "But none of them that have anything to do with rings."

"I hate to sound pessimistic," replied Katie, sighing. "But I'm beginning to think that we'll never solve this mystery and *Der Rabe* will find the formula and destroy us all!"

Jim Fielding turned to look at her, a hint of concern on his face. "You're not giving up, are you?" he asked softly, "because if you lose hope then I'm sure to follow suit. I can't do this without you."

She looked into those gorgeous eyes of his and then looked down at her feet. How could she possibly think of letting him down, not to mention all of humanity? Oh dear.

"Can't do this without me, huh?" she finally said with a grin. "Are you ready to admit that I'm as legitimate a reporter as you, Mr. Fielding?"

He chuckled. "Yes, my dear Miss Porter," he replied. "I am definitely ready to admit that."

They smiled at each other for a moment before Jim suggested that they switch sides of the roof and look east and west. Jim took the east side, which looked out upon the front of the estate. He took note of the circular driveway which was lined with flowerbeds and a smattering of shrubbery.

Katie looked out upon the back of the property. At first, she didn't see it, but soon her eyes fell upon the layout directly underneath and to the front of her.

"Jim…er…Mr. Fielding," she called to him. "Please come here, will you?"

He quickly joined her on the west side of the roof and looked where she pointed.

"See here," she directed. "If we look right, and a few yards away, we see the large fountain."

Jim nodded.

"Now, imagine drawing a line from the back of the house to the fountain," Katie continued. "Now look left. See the stables?"

"Yes," Jim replied. "Just center, about fifty feet west of Mad Uncle Henry Henry's birdhouse."

"That's about right," agreed Katie, her hand and finger still extended. "Draw your imaginary line from the fountain to the stables. Now look all the way left. There's the greenhouse."

"Oh, I see it!" exclaimed Jim. "From the back of the house to the fountain, from the fountain to the stables, from the stables to the greenhouse, and from the greenhouse back to the house forms a giant ring! Miss Porter, I think you've found something!"

"Well, maybe," replied Katie, although she was beaming. "There *is* the circular driveway on the east side as well. Both sides form rings."

"So, I say we search both," recommended Jim. "Let's take the west side first. Something tells me it's the most significant."

"And then the east side, with the driveway," agreed Katie, turning toward the roof's door. "Although I believe that Ruddy would have found it too obvious to hide something as important as the formula in a flowerbed. Why, anyone could accidently find it. Yet, you never know!"

"My thoughts, exactly," replied Jim, nodding. "So, let's start by searching Mad Uncle Henry's birdhouse since it sits right in the middle of our ring and, if needed, we can finish our search in the flowerbeds!"

"Good idea!" said Katie excitedly, as they made their way through the attic.

They had descended the staircase and stepped into the hall when a thought suddenly occurred to Katie. Stepping over and picking up the White's telephone, she placed a call.

"Hello?" she said into the receiver. "E.M. Butler please. Oh, he's not. Do you know what time he'll be in. No? Oh dear. No, no message. Thank you, goodbye."

She hung up and handed the phone to Jim. "Now it's your turn," she said.

He understood immediately. If they could catch someone at home, they could rule that person out as *Der Rabe*, since it would be virtually impossible for him to be digging holes on the Sunset Hill estate at the same time. Luck, however, was not on their side.

"Thank you, no, there's no message," said Jim into the phone receiver. "I'll try him again later."

Turning to Katie, who was standing next to him, Jim said, "Well, it appears that both Mr. Butler and Kenneth are still our only suspects."

"I wonder," replied Katie, somewhat thoughtfully, and taking the phone from Jim, she placed a call to her grandmother at Rosegate.

"Hello, Gran," she said into the phone. "I just wanted to let you know that Mr. Fielding and I are still at Sunset Hill and will be for another hour. Yes, we'll be home well before dark. Yes, Gran. Yes, I know, Gran," she said, glancing up at Jim with a look of resignation on her face. "Listen Gran, is Mr. Henderson there with you? I heard that he was to be released from the hospital very soon and wondered if he had made it to Rosegate?"

There was a pause as Katie listened to her grandmother on the other end of the line. "Oh, I see," she finally said. "No reason, really. But now that I think of it, did you happen to discuss my little cryptogram puzzle with him? You did? How interesting. No, no worries, Gran. I was just wondering. I'll be home soon. Goodbye, Gran."

She hung up the phone and looked at Jim but said nothing. He guessed the truth.

"Mr. Henderson knows about Ruddy's code," he said, and she nodded her head. "And he is not currently at Rosegate."

Katie nodded her head again. "No, he is not," she confirmed with a sigh.

She turned and walked to the library, peeking her head in to find Ruth and Robert sitting on the couch drinking tea and eating cake.

"Robert," Katie said, walking a few steps into the room. "Is Mr. Henderson still in the hospital?"

"No, Katie," he replied. "We released him early this morning. Why?"

"No reason," Katie smiled. "But if you two could tear yourselves away from your cake, and each other, for a minute, Mr. Fielding and I could use your help."

After a brief discussion, it was decided that Ruth and Robert should search the flowerbeds and shrubbery along the circular driveway in front of the house while Jim and Katie searched inside Mad Uncle Henry's birdhouse and the area surrounding it.

Both teams worked for an hour but did not find anything. Completely dejected, they returned to the house for a quick drink of water and to say their goodbyes.

As Katie and Jim began to make their departure out the back door, Mad Uncle Henry came flying toward them. They both ducked as he swooped over their heads, dropping one of his toys at Katie's feet. She picked it up and walked back inside to where Tom was sitting in his wheelchair. The Macaw was perched on Tom's shoulder and gave Katie a whistle as she approached.

"Here, Mad Uncle Henry," she said, holding up the toy to give him. "You dropped your ball."

Instead of taking it from her, Mad Uncle Henry just rocked back and forth repeating "Ruddy's toy, Ruddy's toy."

"Yes, it is," replied Katie, patiently. "Take it or I will put it away in the drawer so nobody else will step on it."

Mad Uncle Henry whistled and squawked but finally took the ball from Katie's outstretched hand and flew out of the window to his birdhouse.

"He doesn't like it very much," sighed Tom, watching as the large bird landed on the perch to his birdhouse and flipped the ball inside. "Ruddy sent it to him from England. Maybe it's popular with Macaw's over there but Mad Uncle Henry seldom plays with it here."

"Yes, I remember seeing the address for the pet shop in Ruddy's wallet," said Katie, walking over and gazing out the open window. "Well, it looks like he'll keep it in his birdhouse for now. Goodbye Tom. Try to stay out of trouble."

"Do I have a choice?" he replied, but Katie barely heard him as she joined Jim outside and they made their way to the stables to collect their horses.

They road back to Rosegate mostly in silence, both frustrated at not finding the formula, or the German spy, and knowing that time was running out.

"Would you like to stay for dinner?" asked Katie, upon their arrival back at Rosegate. Darkness was just beginning to fall as they walked toward the main house.

"No, thank you," replied Jim. "I must get home. I need a hot bath and a good night's sleep after all that scampering around Sunset Hill today. Thank you for an interesting day, Miss Porter," and, with that, he tipped his hat and walked on to his car.

Katie, herself, was exhausted and, shortly after dinner, retired to her bedroom and promptly fell asleep. However, her slumber was restless and filled with anxious dreams.

"I'm going to hand it over to the Surgeon General," Ruddy said in her dream. *"My orders."*

"All rings must be examined," demanded Kenneth.

"Aren't you going to ask me?" E.M.'s face suddenly appearing. *"Ask you what?"* *"If I'm Der Rabe, the escaped leader of the gang?"* he replied. *"Are you?"* she asked.

"Sometimes the only way to gain clarity is to view things a few feet away," said Jim with a smile that was definitely his best feature.

"You're not giving up, are you? Because if you lose hope then I'm sure to follow suit. I can't do this without you."

"Ruddy sent it from England."

"I can't do this without you."

"44-49-55-43-40-53-44-49-42."

"We could see the dent in it where a bullet had hit it, nearly flinging the helmet off his head."

"From England."

"My neighbor had a Raven named Oscar."

"In The Ring."

"E.M. saved every single one of those people. He was awarded the Bronze Star."

"Gran, did you discuss the cryptogram with Mr. Henderson?"

"Something strange is happening and I don't know who to trust."

"I was with the International Red Cross. I speak both French and German."

"From England."

"Don't know who to trust."

"Ruddy sent it."

She jolted awake, sitting straight up in her bed. "Ruddy sent it from England," she whispered to herself.

Katie finally knew where Ruddy's formula was hidden.

CHAPTER 17
TRAPPED!

The clock on her bedside table read four-twenty am as Katie carefully slid out of bed so as not to disturb Nugget who was sleeping soundly beside her. She slipped into a skirt and blouse and pulled a pair of Oxford shoes from the back of her closet.

"I'll need practical shoes for this job," she said to herself. "And perhaps a sweater since the sun isn't up yet."

Waiting to put on her shoes until she got downstairs, Katie quietly descended the staircase in her stocking feet. When she reached the hallway, she realized that she should leave her grandmother a note and tore a small sheet of paper from the pad that lay next to the telephone. Two small sheets came off in her hands by accident and she unconsciously folded the second one and stuffed it into the pocket of her skirt.

"Gone to Sunset Hill on an important mission," was all she wrote on the remaining sheet, signing it "Love, Katie." She walked to the dining room and placed it at her grandmother's place at the breakfast table.

Then she put on her shoes and sweater and proceeded through the mud room where she grabbed a flashlight before exiting out the back door toward the garage.

The stars were still bright above her in the night sky as she drove through the quiet dark streets to Sunset Hill.

"I know I should have called Jim or E.M. for back-up, just in case," she said to herself. "But it's only four-fifty am and I'm sure they're still asleep," she rationalized. "Besides, *Der Rabe* is most likely in bed himself so I should be fairly safe."

Her nerves were tingling in excited anticipation as she turned into the large entrance to the estate.

When she was nearing the top of the circular drive, she flicked off the headlights on the MG, and then turned off the engine, rolling silently toward the front of the house and gliding to a stop.

Pausing to make sure she hadn't awakened any of the family, she stepped out of the car, and quietly pushed the door shut, reaching for the flashlight and taking it with her. She snuck around the side of the mansion and toward the back yard. There she clicked on the flashlight and proceeded carefully to Mad Uncle Henry's birdhouse.

She was not surprised to find the birdhouse empty of the Macaw. The bird usually slept on a perch in a corner of the hallway in the house. She placed the flashlight on the ground and reached up to feel inside the little birdhouse. Unfortunately, she found that, even on tiptoes, she was not tall enough to fully reach inside. She looked around for something to stand on and saw, leaning against the greenhouse, a small step ladder.

"Perfect," she whispered and, picking up the flashlight, made her way over to the ladder, grabbing it with one hand and dragging it back to the middle of the yard where the birdhouse stood.

She opened the ladder and carefully climbed up, the flashlight in one hand, as she braced herself with the other. This time she reached the top and could easily see inside, finding Mad Uncle Henry's house filled with toys. The ball that Ruddy had sent from England was near the front edge. Katie picked it up and quickly stepped back down the ladder.

"Now to see if I'm right," she murmured. She propped the flashlight on one of the rungs of the ladder so that she could better examine the ball in the light and began to turn the small toy over in her hand. She noticed that the ball was made up of two halves held together. "I wonder if there is some way to…" she whispered, and grasping the ball tightly, gave it a strong twist, causing the two halves of the ball to start to separate. She continued to unscrew the top of the ball from its bottom until both halves lay in her hand. And, just as she had expected, the inside of the toy was hollow and there, folded into a tiny square, was a piece of paper.

Katie gasped and, lifting it out, quickly unfolded the paper to reveal the prized formula. Without stopping to study it more closely, she started to screw Mad Uncle Henry's toy back together.

"I'll take that now!" said a firm male voice behind her.

Startled, she jumped and spun around, knocking the ladder over, the flashlight crashing to the ground where it promptly clicked off. Now standing in darkness, she strained her eyes to see who was standing before her.

"You've saved me quite a lot of trouble, Katie Porter," said the shadowy figure, one hand extended out toward her, the other holding the handle of a shovel. "I might have had to dig for days, but now you've found it for me. Put the ball down on the ground in front of you and back away slowly!"

"The only way you're getting this ball is over my dead body, Mr. West," she exclaimed, with as much courage as she could muster. She put her arms behind her back, gripping the ball tightly in her right hand.

"Yes, well, that was part of my plan anyway, Miss Porter," replied Kenneth, calmly. "After all, I can't afford to leave behind any witnesses."

"Is that why you tried to kill Adolpho Henderson?" asked Katie, stalling for time. Surely someone in the house would awaken and come to investigate the commotion in the backyard. "Did he recognize you at my dinner party and you were afraid that he would identify you?"

"Adolpho Henderson! Ha!" replied Kenneth West, throwing back his head and letting out a mock laugh. "That little man! His real name is Adolph Henrick. He is an inconsequential shoe salesman from Bavaria. He still holds a grudge against me because I had his entire family executed."

"You what!" exclaimed Katie, shocked, with panic rising in her chest.

"Casualties of war, my dear Katie," replied Kenneth with a shrug. "They were Jews. And it's not as though I personally pulled the trigger," he added, lifting the shovel high above his shoulder, ready to strike her. "I just gave the order."

"You are a monster," she cried, her voice shaking. "How could you serve your country and still betray it!"

"I have not betrayed *my* country, Fraulein," Kenneth replied proudly, now bringing down the shovel to rest upon his shoulder. "I have been, and continue to be, a loyal servant of the Third Reich!"

"But you were a soldier with the U.S. Army and a member of Ruddy's platoon?" said Katie, confused. "I don't understand."

"I am a Major in the German Army, silly woman!" he sneered. "And, as *Der Rabe*, one of my country's greatest spies."

"But why work with the US Army to capture your own gang and get possession of a chemical formula that you already had?" asked Katie, still puzzled. None of this made any sense.

"Ah, well, since you are about to die, I will tell you," he chuckled. "I was in Berlin when I found out that the members of my own spy ring had betrayed me. They had found the chemical formula and, without my knowledge, were planning on selling it to the highest bidder and splitting the proceeds among themselves. I needed to punish them and, by doing so, take possession of the formula."

Katie strained her ears, hoping to hear signs that members of the White family might be waking. Unfortunately, there was only the voice of *Der Rabe* as he continued his sordid tale.

"Then, quite by luck, German Intelligence picked up signals that an invasion might be imminent in Sicily, where my gang was in hiding. I realized I wouldn't have time to get to Licata and hunt them down, so I came up with a plan to infiltrate one of the army units that would be involved in the invasion. No one would suspect an American soldier in the middle of a battle," Kenneth West chuckled sardonically. "I could hunt down my gang at leisure. All I needed was the assistance of the good Colonel Diggins. I told him that he would be getting a cut of the money when the formula was sold. He was a very willing accomplice. In fact, it was he who came up with the secret plan to capture my own gang for me, with the unwitting help of Ruddy and Jim, and, at the same time, recover the formula! It was absolutely brilliant!"

"He's completely mad," thought Katie to herself, all the while looking for an opportunity to escape.

"But your Ruddy had to interfere," Kenneth continued, now pacing back and forth. "He was supposed to hand the formula over to Diggins, but he kept having second thoughts. He ended up sending it here to Sunset Hill after Diggins was found dead. Said he couldn't trust anyone, anymore."

"Did you kill Colonel Diggins?" asked Katie, suspecting the truth but not really wanting to hear the answer.

"Did I kill him?" scoffed Kenneth. "Yes, of course. Diggins started demanding a bigger cut. In the end, I had to shoot him. We have no use for a weak, greedy man in our new grand empire. Because, of course, the formula is not for sale. It will be used to bring the world to its knees in submission and the Reich will rise again!"

Katie stood still for a moment. "Poor Ruddy," she thought. "He was trying to do the right thing by preserving the formula and sending it home."

She looked over at Kenneth and said firmly, "The war is over, *Der Rabe*, and the Axis has been defeated. The world is free. You will not get the formula from me. You have failed. You might as well put down the shovel and give yourself up! Several people know where I am, and they are already bringing the police!" she added with false bravado, knowing that the whole story was a lie. How foolish she had been to come alone!

Kenneth West grinned and put his hand to his ear pretending to listen. "I think not, Katie Porter," he taunted. "No one is coming to save you, but it was a good try. Now, you will place the ball with the formula down on the ground in front of you or I will kill you and take it!"

"You plan to kill me anyway so I will not..." Katie started to say but suddenly, from out of the darkness, came a loud screech and the flapping of large wings upon the head of Kenneth West.

He let out a startled yell, dropping the shovel, and shielding his face with his hands. Mad Uncle Henry stopped flapping, rose up into the air, circled around, and swooped down again upon the cowering man.

Katie used the bird's diversion to try and escape. She turned quickly on her heels and ran as fast as she could, her heart pounding in her throat, knowing that her life depended on it. She saw the greenhouse a short distance in front of her and she made a dash for it, the ball still gripped tightly in her hand.

She heard Mad Uncle Henry squawk loudly, and, glancing over her shoulder, could see him continue to swoop upon Kenneth, until the man was able to pick up the shovel and swing it at the bird, thwarting the attack. Mad Uncle Henry then retreated, flying quickly toward the main house.

"I hope he's gone for help," she said to herself as she neared the greenhouse, sensing that Kenneth was now closing in on her. "If only I can get to it before he catches me. I'll lock myself in and wait until help arrives."

However, just as she reached the greenhouse and pulled open the door, Kenneth was upon her, grabbing her arm and holding her tightly.

"Caught you!" he snarled. "I'll take that, if you don't mind!" and he grabbed the ball from her hand, dropping it into his pocket. He threw Katie roughly into the greenhouse and slammed the door shut behind her, sliding the lock in place. She heard him laugh and yell, "Miss Porter, you've made a very grave mistake! In greenhouses, the lock is on the outside, not the inside! I hope you don't get too terribly hot in there!"

"No need to worry about me!" Katie bravely yelled back at him, although she was, in fact, scared out of her wits. "I'll find a way out of here in no time."

"I hope you do," Kenneth laughed. "Because I'm going to set the place on fire. Just to keep things interesting!"

She looked out of the window and saw him walking quickly away. He reached into his pocket and pulled out the ball, unscrewing it make sure the formula was tucked inside. Seeing the paper there, he quickly screwed the ball back together and, giving it a kiss, dropped it back into his pocket. Then he disappeared into the woods.

Katie wasn't going to wait to see if he would return. She pulled and pushed at the glass door of the greenhouse. It would not budge. She yelled and pounded her fists on it. This only served to wear her out and bruise her hands.

She decided to take a run at it, hoping that the impact of her weight would be heavy enough against the lock to break it. But, as she was stepping back in preparation, she saw Kenneth returning. He held a gas can and was approaching the side of the greenhouse, pouring a stream of gas behind him. He continued pouring gas along the side of the building before turning and continuing the gas stream down the middle of the lawn, finally stopping at the base of Mad Uncle Henry's birdhouse. He then dropped the can, and, after patting his vest pockets, brought out a book of matches. With one last look at the greenhouse, he struck a match and threw it into the gas stream, catching it on fire. He watched for a few minutes as the fire progressed up the stream and then took off at a run.

In horror, Katie watched through the glass door as the flames approached the greenhouse. In a moment, the building would be engulfed in flames. She tugged, again, at the door handle, but it still would not budge.

"I'm in a glass house," she reminded herself. "All I have to do is break one of the panes and climb out."

She looked around but found nothing but flowerpots and bags of soil, which she had little hope would work. She tried anyway, and hurled several pots at the glass walls, which only succeeded in their crashing to the floor and breaking. The glass remained intact.

The fire reached the corner of the greenhouse and, with the help of some small bushes that surrounded it, the wooden trusses of the tiny building burst into flames. Smoke filled the inside of the structure and Katie began choking.

"There must be a way out of here!" she exclaimed. "I refuse to die like this!" However, she knew there was little hope as she felt herself succumb to the effects of the smoke.

The last thing she could remember before losing consciousness was the sound of an axe breaking through the door of the greenhouse.

"Katie? Katie?" she heard a familiar male voice calling through the clearing fog in her mind. "Can you hear me?"

She slowly opened her eyes to see Jim Fielding's looking deep into her own. He had an anxious expression on his face, which changed into one of relief once he realized that she was alive.

"Mr. Fielding!" exclaimed Katie. "How did you get here?"

"Ruthie called us," he explained, nodded over to Katie's friend, who was standing close by with an ax in her hands. "We've been busy saving your life, but I can explain everything in more detail once we move farther away from this fire."

Now fully awake, Katie realized that she was lying partially on the ground with the upper half of her body cradled in Jim Fielding's arms. As she looked over his shoulder, she could see the greenhouse engulfed in flames. They were only a few feet away and the heat was radiating off them.

Ruth had tears running down her face as she quietly put down the ax and walked over to clasp her best friend's hand.

"Can you walk, Katie?" she asked, softly. "We really must go. The greenhouse is about to collapse."

Katie nodded as Ruth and Jim helped her to her feet. She now became aware that people were running about and shouting and there were sounds of firetrucks racing up the driveway.

As they turned to move away from the fire, Katie suddenly stopped as if remembering something. She reached into her pocket and brought out a small slip of paper, holding it up briefly for Jim to see, before turning and walking back to the burning building. He followed close behind her and then watched as Katie silently crumpled it up and tossed it into the flames. They stood together, Jim's hands on Katie's shoulders, as it burned into ashes before they turned and walked back to join Ruth waiting at a safe distance away.

Dawn was breaking as the firefighters fought to put out the flames. They could not save the greenhouse, but they did stop the fire from spreading to the nearby woods, the main house, and Mad Uncle Henry's birdhouse.

Feeling grateful to be alive, Katie looked out to the horizon as the sun rose, its rays just peeking over the tree lined hill.

"*Nescit occasum sol montis*," she murmured softly, her arms folded, her hands pulling her sweater tightly around her.

"The sunset knows the hill," smiled Jim, standing next to her.

Katie smiled back at him. "In this case, the sunrise, Jim Fielding. Definitely, the sunrise!"

CHAPTER 18
ALL IS EXPLAINED

"My only regret is that he got away," lamented Katie, as she sat in the White's Livingroom, sipping a cup of hot tea.

She had just come down from Ruth's room where she had enjoyed a quick bath and a change of clothes, supplied from her friend's closet. Now she happily sat, safe and sound, surrounded by friendly faces.

Mr. Henderson had finally arrived at Rosegate that very morning, having spent the time after his release from the hospital buying a new set of clothes for his stay with the Porters. Upon his arrival, Katie's grandmother had asked him to drive her over to Sunset Hill to see what mischief her granddaughter had managed to get into and they were shocked to see the extent of the fire and hear about the adventure that had caused it.

All those who had been involved with the case were assembled in the room, with the exception of Poppy and Mrs. White, who were in Washington for a luncheon with the First Lady of the United States. Ruth had called her father that morning to tell him about the fire but assured him that there was no need for her parents to rush home as everything was now under control.

"But he didn't get away," replied E.M. Butler, who was standing by a window, gazing out in the direction of the destroyed greenhouse. "He's been arrested and is in local police custody, awaiting the arrival of the FBI. He'll most likely stand trial in the International Court of Justice in the Hague."

"But how…?" stammered Katie, looking at E.M. and then to the others seated around the room.

"Perhaps you and Mr. Fielding should start at the beginning," Mrs. Porter said calmly, now that Katie was out of danger. "That might help us put together all of the pieces."

"That sounds like my cue," smiled Jim, from his chair next to Katie's. He took a deep breath and began. "I suppose it all started during the war when a small group of us were recruited by Colonel Diggins to capture a dangerous spy ring and find a powerful chemical formula. This formula had the potential to cure several types of cancer, but it could also be used to create a massive bomb."

Hearing this, everyone in the room gasped.

"We succeeded in our mission," continued Jim. "But then an argument broke out between the six of us. Three of us wanted the formula destroyed and the other three, including Ruddy, wanted to preserve it. Since Ruddy was the team leader, his decision won out and he took possession of it for the remainder of our time in Sicily. Later, when I asked him whether he had handed the formula over to the colonel, he told me that he hadn't but that the formula was as safe as the crown jewels. Colonel Diggins had been killed, you see, and then Ruddy came to feel that he couldn't trust anyone. He ended up sending the formula home to Sunset Hill."

Katie now picked up the story, "it was Colonel Diggins who arranged for Kenneth West, a German Army Major and notorious spy, to infiltrate Ruddy's platoon. *Der Rabe* was among you the entire time," she added, turning to Jim.

"Even up until yesterday," Jim replied, shaking his head in disgust. "And I was helping him! It's hard to believe! I had no idea," he added sadly.

"Ruddy's plan was to travel to Washington, D.C. when he was home on leave," continued Katie, blushing slightly at the memory of their planned elopement, news she hadn't been able to share yet. "And hand the formula over to the Surgeon General, himself. But then his leave was cancelled..."

"and he wasn't sure if he would ever make it home," interjected Ruth. "So, he sent Katie and me a clue, in the form of a number's code at the bottom of some letters, telling us where to find the formula."

"Except he did such a good job with the code that it took us this long to figure it out," said Katie, smiling. "All this time the formula was hidden in Mad Uncle Henry's toy."

"We should have figured that out sooner," nodded Jim. "How else could he have sent the formula home, and have it hidden without help from someone here? He would not have wanted to put that person at risk should *Der Rabe* discover what he had done."

"So, he enlisted the help of Mad Uncle Henry," Tom said, chuckling. "The perfect partner. He knew that Mad Uncle Henry would discard the ball in his birdhouse because Ruddy, himself, had taught him the trick."

"All Ruddy had to do was create the short "In The Ring" clue," said E.M., snapping his fingers. "Because the birdhouse sits in the middle of a ring of structures in Sunset Hill's backyard."

"Mad Uncle Henry was the perfect partner in more ways than one," added Katie. "It was he who first tried to save me. If he hadn't attacked Kenneth West when he did, giving me a chance to escape, I would have surely been killed on the spot."

"But he only delayed the threat," her grandmother pointed out. "You almost died in the fire."

"Yes, I meant to ask about that," asked Katie, turning and addressing Jim. "How did you manage to appear just in the nick of time to break down the door with an axe and haul me out of there?"

"I didn't" replied Jim. "Well, I did haul you out, but it was Ruth who broke down the door with the axe."

"Ruthie?" exclaimed Katie, now turning in the other direction to face her friend.

"When your grandmother called me at five am," began Ruth, smiling. "I knew something was up."

"I had awoken at four forty-five, and, fortunately, gazed out the window just in time to see you drive away," interjected Mrs. Porter. "I went downstairs and found your note. Worried that you might end up in trouble, I telephoned Ruth to let her know you were on your way."

"Gran!" exclaimed Katie, smiling affectionately at her grandmother. "I'm so glad that you did!"

"After I got off the phone with your grandmother," continued Ruth. "I called E.M."

"Fortunately, she got hold of me. I had just arrived home after being out of town attending a friend's wedding. I hadn't even made it to bed yet. I called Mr. Fielding," E.M. added, nodding at Jim. "And we assembled the troops, as one would say in wartime."

"We jumped in our cars," added Jim. "And drove over as quickly as we could."

"Meanwhile, I woke Tom and we watched from the upstairs window. We could see you running from someone and Mad Uncle Henry flying toward the house to get help," explained Ruth. "Tom called the police while I ran downstairs just in time to see the greenhouse catch fire."

"After I got off the phone with the police, I hopped down the stairs just in time to see Mr. West running across the back yard," said Tom, joining in. "I knew I had to stop him somehow, so I hopped out the porch door and threw myself down on the ground directly in front of him. He was so intent on escaping that he didn't see me and fell over my cast."

"Which was fortunate because it slowed Kenneth down long enough to give me time to tackle him as he was picking himself up and racing for the corner of the house," said E.M. grinning broadly. "I don't mind telling you that I completely enjoyed taking him down, the swine!"

"We could see the flames billowing up from somewhere behind the mansion, so I ran past E.M. and Kenneth, rounded the corner of the house, and ran toward the greenhouse," said Jim, picking up the story. "I thought I was too late until I saw Ruth."

"I could just barely see you through the smoky glass panes as you were trying to break out of the greenhouse, Katie, and knew that there wasn't a second to spare," said Ruth, a frown crossing her face. "So, I grabbed our axe from the woodpile and managed to break down the door just as Mr. Fielding arrived."

"I jumped in and carried you out," said Jim, softly.

"So, you all saved me!" cried Katie, looking around the room. "How will I ever thank you!"

"For my part," said Tom, shrugging his shoulders. "I was just returning the favor."

"The police arrived just behind the firetrucks and took Mr. West into custody," said E.M. "I told them that he was an arsonist but that you and Mr. Fielding would be down later this afternoon to give them the rest of the charges! But before he was taken away, I managed to reach into his pocket and reclaim this," and, reaching into his own pants pocket, he pulled out Mad Uncle Henry's ball.

Everyone gasped as E.M. held it up for a moment before gently tossing it to Katie.

"Great job, E.M." exclaimed Katie, catching the ball with one hand. "Now I will show you how Ruddy hid the formula." She grasped the toy tightly in both hands and unscrewed the top from the bottom. Inside was a slip of paper. "As you can see, the inside of the ball is hollow," she explained, tilting the ball so that everyone could see. "Ruddy simply folded the formula up into a tiny square and tucked it inside. Since he often sent toys to Mad Uncle Henry, no one would have suspected this one when it arrived. It was actually very clever!"

"Ah, the formula," Jim said thoughtfully, glancing over at the slip of paper laying inside the bottom half of the toy. "The embodiment of humanity's struggle between good and evil."

Everyone sat in chilled silence for several minutes, pondering his words.

"Ruddy representing good," Ruth finally remarked. "And Kenneth West representing evil."

"Remember, each side had help," warned Katie. "Ruddy was relying on us, Ruthie, and Kenneth had the help of Colonel Diggins, although his was more a matter of greed than evil."

"The love of money is the root of all evil," whispered Mr. Henderson, looking down at his hands.

"So, what do we do with it now?" asked Tom, as if the paper might explode any minute in Katie's hands.

"With what?" asked Katie, glancing over at him.

"The formula, my future wife," exclaimed Tom, pointing to Katie's lap. "The one you are holding!"

"Oh, this isn't the formula," Katie replied with a smile. She pulled out the thin piece of paper and, unfolding it, held it up for all to see.

"Why, there's nothing on it," cried Ruth, puzzled.

"That looks like it came off of our telephone pad at home, Katie," replied Mrs. Porter, equally puzzled.

"You are correct, Gran! It, in fact, is from our phone pad," responded Katie, still smiling.

"I don't understand," said E.M. "Didn't you just tell us that Ruddy had hidden the formula in the ball?"

"He did," replied Katie, nodding. "And I removed it."

Her friends looked at her, confusion on their faces.

"I had just slipped the formula into my pocket," she explained. "And had not quite screwed the ball back together again when Mr. West snuck up on me. While he was threatening my life, I happened to remember the extra piece of paper I had accidently torn from the phone pad when I wrote the note to Gran. I had shoved it into my pocket on my way out the door at Rosegate. Kenneth West was so intent on telling me about his glorious war record that he didn't notice me sliding my hand into my pocket and bringing the paper out, hidden in the palm of my hand. Then, while I was stalling for time, I put both hands behind my back, giving me the opportunity to place the blank phone pad paper into the ball and screw it back together."

"You took an awful risk, Miss Porter," remarked Jim, but there was a great amount of respect in his voice.

"No more so than coming face-to-face with *Der Rabe*," replied Katie. "It was my only chance of making sure he didn't get the formula. At one point, after locking me inside the greenhouse, I saw him look inside the ball. But he never lifted out the paper and unfolded it. He just assumed it was the formula," Katie added, shaking her head at the thought.

"So, where is it?" asked her grandmother. "What do you do now? Are you going up to Washington to hand it over to the Surgeon General?"

"No, Gran," replied her granddaughter, softly. "Because I don't have it anymore. It's gone."

"What?" shouted everyone in the room, their chins dropping.

"Katie burned it," replied Jim Fielding calmly. "She threw it in the flames of the greenhouse. We watched it burn to ashes together."

Katie nodded and looked around the room, but no one spoke.

"Perhaps it's for the best," remarked her grandmother, finally.

"Yes, perhaps," agreed Katie, and then, taking a deep breath, she said, "there is something more I need to tell you."

"There's more?" exclaimed Tom, bringing a hand to his forehead in mock despair.

Katie smiled shyly, "Yes, I'm afraid so. I should have told you a long time ago but, somehow, it seemed unimportant after Ruddy was killed."

Ruth smiled and, leaning over, took hold of Katie's hand. "We know, Katie," she said, gently.

"You do?" replied Katie, puzzled.

"Yes," Ruth answered. "Ruddy wrote to me and told me about your planned elopement. He was worried that our families would be angry and might, somehow, take it out on you. He loved you very much, so he asked me to help smooth things over. Poppy and Mother weren't thrilled about the plan, but they understood. Besides, it meant the you would be our sister that much sooner, although you've always been that to us, anyway."

"And I couldn't wait to gain a new grandson," replied Mrs. Porter, giving Katie an affectionate wink.

Startled, Katie stared in disbelief at her grandmother and then back at Ruth. With tears in her eyes, she asked, "but you never said anything? After all this time, you never once asked me about it?"

"It seemed unimportant after Ruddy was killed," replied Ruth, gravely. "And whether you had married during the war, or after it, wouldn't have changed anything. We know that you loved him, and that's the important thing."

"Breakfast is served, Miss Ruth," announced the dignified Ambrose, saving Katie from further discussion. Relieved to have the case finally over, the weary and very hungry group jumped to their feet and followed him to the dining room.

Just after noon, Jim Fielding and Katie went to the Fairfield Police Station to press local charges against Kenneth West, and to inform the FBI of the international crimes that he had committed. Their visit took two hours, but, in the end, Kenneth would be put on the fast track to justice. International authorities were thankful that *Der Rabe* had finally been captured and would stand trial in the Hague. Mr. Adolpho Henderson was asked to fly to the Netherlands to be one of the main witnesses.

"The story's yours," said Jim Fielding, his hands in his pockets as he and Katie left the police station and walked across the street to their cars.

"You're not going to write it for the *Middleton Times*?" Katie asked him, surprised.

"No, I think not," he answered, shaking his head. "It will work better for the *Fairfield Gazette*. And, besides, you cracked the case. You deserve to write the story." He stopped to open the door of Katie's MG. "It's also Captain Rutherford White's story," he added, as she slid behind the wheel. "And who better to write it than his fiancée?"

"O.K.," she replied. "Thank you. But I'll need to know whether you want your name noted as Mr. James Fielding or Jim Fielding of the

Middleton Times," she teased, looking up at him.

"Just Jim," he replied softly, tipping his hat as he turned toward his car, quickly disappearing around the corner.

Katie drove to the *Gazette* and wrote the story. She left nothing out, beginning with the war, and Jim Fielding and the dangerous Kenneth West. She wrote about the White Family and about Mad Uncle Henry, how she and E.M. had worked together to investigate the case, her discovery of the formula, of nearly dying in the fire, and of being rescued by Ruth and Jim.

And she mostly wrote about Ruddy.

She wrote the story from her heart, completing it in just under two hours. Then she carried it to Mr. Connor's office and held her breath as he read it.

After he was finished, the editor looked over at her and sat stunned for several minutes.

"My dear Miss Porter," he said, finally. "Is all of this true?

"Every last word of it," she replied, her hand clasping the locket around her neck.

"Well, my new ace reporter, great job!" he said, smiling warmly at her. "Yours will be our lead story for tomorrow's front page," he added, standing and extending his hand to shake hers. "And I'm certain with a story like this one, our readership will quadruple! I'm going to send Midge out to Sunset Hill right now to take a few pictures to go along with it. Do you think Mad Uncle Henry would mind posing?"

It was late that night, as she was getting ready for bed, that Katie opened her desk drawer and took out her journal. She had made a habit of writing in it every night, even when she was as exhausted as she was this night.

Long ago, she had decided to address each entry as if she were writing a letter to her mother. It had been more important to her when she was a young child than as the young adult she was now. Still, with her mother constantly far away, Katie found it helpful to imagine them having what would ordinarily be a real mother-daughter conversation.

"Dear mother," Katie began,

"Early this morning, I saved the world. Well, I think I did. I won't ever be sure, of course. I could have actually done more harm than good. There is also the possibility that, by destroying the formula, I have just delayed the inevitable, whatever the inevitable turns out to be.

After all, another copy of the formula may still exist or sometime, in the future, someone else may come up with the same one or something similar.

All I can say is that I hope they use it for good and not evil, because after going through a world war to save much of humanity, it would be nice if humanity lasted for a while.

I have come to realize that some problems are not easy to figure out and this makes finding the answers, and making the right choices, very difficult.

But, for now, I believe I have made the right one.
Katie."

~ The End ~

ABOUT THE AUTHOR

K.T. McGivens is best known as a poet and her poems have been published in newspapers, community publications, and anthologies. She has written six books of poetry and is currently working on an anthology of her best works with a target date for publication on Amazon by late October 2019.

She has now ventured into the world of mystery novels and has begun writing a series of short mystery novels featuring her character Katie Porter. The novels are geared toward young adults and focus on strong female characters, problem solving, trusted friendships, and tenacity; a formula she learned from growing up reading the Nancy Drew Mysteries.

Ms. McGivens grew up in Maryland and earned both a Bachelor's Degree and a Master's Degree from the University of Maryland. She now lives in the panhandle of Florida.

Made in the USA
Monee, IL
19 February 2020

21936493R00079